A Sting in the Tale

A Thrilling Comedy in Two Acts

Brian Clemens
and Dennis Spooner

A SAMUEL FRENCH ACTING EDITION

SAMUELFRENCH.COM
SAMUELFRENCH-LONDON.CO.UK

MUSIC USE NOTE

Licensees are solely responsible for obtaining formal written permission from copyright owners to use copyrighted music in the performance of this play and are strongly cautioned to do so. If no such permission is obtained by the licensee, then the licensee must use only original music that the licensee owns and controls. Licensees are solely responsible and liable for all music clearances and shall indemnify the copyright owners of the play(s) and their licensing agent, Samuel French, against any costs, expenses, losses and liabilities arising from the use of music by licensees. Please contact the appropriate music licensing authority in your territory for the rights to any incidental music.

IMPORTANT BILLING AND CREDIT REQUIREMENTS

If you have obtained performance rights to this title, please refer to your licensing agreement for important billing and credit requirements.

A STING IN THE TALE

First presented by arrangement with Michael Codron at the Yvonne Arnaud Theatre, Guildford, on 11th May, 1982, with the following cast of characters:

Nigel Forbes	Jack Douglas
Max Goodman	Pete Murray
Jill Prentice	Marguerite Hardiman
Ann Forbes	Dilys Laye
Detective Inspector Berry	Bill Pertwee

The play directed by Val May
Setting by Graham Brown
Lighting by James Baird

This revised version subsequently presented at the Theatre Royal, Windsor, on 21st February, 1984, with the following cast of characters:

Nigel Forbes	Jack Douglas
Max Goodman	Richard Kay
Jill Prentice	Su Douglas
Ann Forbes	Rosemarie Dunham
Detective Inspector Berry	Davyd Harries

The play directed by Hugh Goldie
Setting by John Page
Lighting by Neil Goodwill

The action of the play takes place in Nigel Forbes' study in his country house in Oxfordshire, over one weekend

ACT I SCENE 1 Saturday morning
       SCENE 2 Some time later
       SCENE 3 That night

ACT II SCENE 1 Sunday morning
        SCENE 2 That night

Time – the present

SYNOPSIS OF SCENES

The section of the play takes place in Nigel Forbes' study in his country house in Oxfordshire, over one week-end.

ACT I

Scene 1   Saturday morning
Scene 2   Some time later
Scene 3   That night

ACT II

Scene 1   Sunday morning
Scene 2   That night

A Sting in the Tale

*THE CURTAIN RISES ON: NIGEL FORBES' Study.
It is Saturday Morning.*

*It was probably once the drawing room of this large,
oldish house, set somewhere in isolated Oxfordshire.*

*Up stage, and placed left of centre, french windows lead
out onto a terrace and garden beyond. What we can
see of the garden suggests that it is overgrown, and
somewhat neglected.*

*Stage right, a door leads to the hallway, and the other
rooms of the house.*

*Near to the door is a large, excellent quality desk. The
desk is very neat; a telephone, an antique desk lamp,
neatly stacked papers, an antique paper knife, and an
electric typewriter. Behind this desk is a good quality
swing chair, some built-in shelves. These shelves
contain books, interspaced with objets d'art, and a
tape recorder.*

*Stage left is a cheap, folding-type table, with an equally
cheap bentwood chair. This table serves as a desk
too, but it is very untidy. It is cluttered with papers,
jam jars containing pencils, and a tatty manual typewriter. Beneath the table a cheap tin waste basket is
filled almost to overflowing.*

*Elsewhere in the area is a sofa; a small fridge with a tray
of bottles and glasses on top of it, and—downstage*

centre — an antique chest. There is also at least one easy chair in the area.

Framed, theatrical posters, of various productions of FORBES and GOODMAN's plays adorn the walls.

The impression is of a lived-in, worked-in, office. No-one has designed the layout, it has just 'happened' over some years.

At this moment the drapes are drawn across the french windows, and the room is lit by overhead light, and by the desk lamp on FORBES' desk.

As the CURTAIN RISES we HEAR the sounds of the countryside at night. The hooting of an owl. There is the rumble of thunder in the air.

NIGEL FORBES is alone on stage.

NIGEL FORBES is anything over forty five or so, a tall, well set-up, attractive man, with an almost languid, cultured drawl that adds to his enormous — albeit cultivated — charm. He is always immaculate, and dresses with great taste.

FORBES — wearing gloves — crosses to his desk. He picks up a document, and his spectacles (which are almost always to be found on his desk) and — without even putting them on — he holds them, and squints through the lens at the document. Satisfied, he places the document back on the desk projecting from under a blotting pad. He returns his spectacles to his desk.

GOODMAN — Enters the study through the door that leads to the hallway.

MAX GOODMAN is a complete contrast to his partner. He is smallish, his hair either thinning or ill cut. He is around forty years of age, and has an almost neurotic nervous energy. His clothes are casual and ill-matched. A loose red cardigan, a yellow shirt, and green socks.

GOODMAN—also wearing gloves—is tense, and this tends to manifest itself in an air of excitement.

GOODMAN. O.K., Nije. We're ready.

FORBES. You unlocked the side door?

GOODMAN. Yes. We haven't overlooked a thing.

FORBES. Excellent, Max. Excellent. (*FORBES picks up a knife from his desk, and offers it to GOODMAN— who regards it for a moment.*) Come on, take it. We agreed that you should do it. (*GOODMAN takes the knife reluctantly.*)

GOODMAN. God, I'm nervous. What if it doesn't work?

FORBES. It's got to work—for both our sakes. Now, come on, Max — motivate. We have been in the grip of a ruthless blackmailer far too long. And in a few moments he'll be coming through that door . . . (*At this moment we HEAR a car draw up outside. They react.*) That's him! (*Immediately, between them, they switch off the lights, and—in the darkness—take up positions of hiding. Now HEAR the doorbell ring. A few moments, then it rings again.*) (*whispers*) He thinks the house is empty. . . . He'll make his way to the side door.

GOODMAN. (*whispers*) I'm still nervous!

FORBES. (*whispers*) Ssssh . . . We're nearly there. He's found the side door unlocked. . . . He's in the house now—coming down the hall . . . and in a few moments. . . .

(*The handle of the drawing room door rattles a fraction, and the door slowly starts to open. A MAN enters carrying a torch. He wears a full beard, snap brim hat, coat with collar turned up, plus gloves. He moves to start searching the drawers of FORBES' desk. Then, finally, he spotlights—with his torch—the document slipped under the blotting pad. He reaches for it, and — as he slowly slides it out — so FORBES and GOODMAN attack him. FORBES grapples with, and holds the MAN, and turns him so that GOODMAN can stab him twice. The MAN falls to the floor — dead! Working as a practiced team FORBES and GOODMAN pick up the body, carry it over to the antique chest, and place it inside. GOOD-MAN hurries over to switch on the desk lamp, and look to where FORBES is just closing the lid of the chest.)*

GOODMAN. I did it! It was easier than I thought.

FORBES. (*He shakes his head, and moves away from the chest.*) It's no good, Max. We're not going to get away with it . . .

GOODMAN. What? Why, Nije—everything went as planned . . . (*At this moment there is a loud knocking from within the chest! GOODMAN and FORBES move to open it and the 'MAN' sits up— 'he' is actually JILL PRENTICE their attractive secretary.*)

JILL. Have you finished? Or do I get buried under the summer house now?

FORBES. We've finished for the moment, Jill. We'll have coffee at the usual time

JILL. Right. . . . (*She removes her hat and beard, steps out of the chest, closes the lid, and Exits. At the same time FORBES moves to pull aside the drapes covering the french windows, and — as sunshine floods in — we realise it is day.*)

GOODMAN. Nije? What did we overlook?

FORBES. What did we overlook? The critics, Max. And our audience. (*The night sounds of the owl, and thunder, are again HEARD. FORBES moves to the tape recorder and switches it off.*) The plot is banal. Totally unacceptable.

GOODMAN. But we can't throw away three months hard work.

FORBES. It would be laughed off the stage.

GOODMAN. Perhaps we should change it into a comedy then?

FORBES. That isn't our field, Max. We're thriller writers.

GOODMAN. We're the only ones who remember that. We haven't had a hit in years.

FORBES. Well, let me assure you — this one isn't even a near miss. (*He picks up a sheaf of papers from his desk as he speaks, and hands them to GOODMAN.*)

GOODMAN. You're right of course. It is terrible. (*He tears up the pages, and deposits them in his overflowing waste basket.*) But what do you expect? Our early plays are out of fashion — the amateur rights drying up. . . . You know damn well I've got a great tax bill looming over me — creditors piling up — and starting to get nasty. How can I be expected to work under such pressures?

FORBES. I am in exactly the same boat, Max. My tax bill is even larger than yours — my creditors more numerous — and nastier! I'm only just managing to keep up appearances, and clinging to this house by the skin of my teeth. But for the fact that Ann has some money of her own, I would have sunk without trace months ago.

GOODMAN. And who's fault's that, Nije? Who said let's get rid of our agent and save ten per cent? Who said he could handle all our business affairs?

FORBES. Oh dear, all this bickering — it only confirms what I've been thinking for some time now. That we should call it a day.

GOODMAN. Eh?

FORBES. Max, undeniably over the years our writing collaboration has brought us a measure of success, adulation, fame, money, and even one good review from Milton Shulman — but equally undeniably the creative spirit that once sparked between us appears to have died. (*GOODMAN appears that he is about to protest, but:*) No, Max, hear me out. I'm not apportioning blame — indeed, I am willing to accept the brunt of it upon my own shoulders . . . but perhaps it is, quite simply, like a once fruitful marriage that is no longer working — time for a divorce.

GOODMAN. You can't be serious. You and me split up?

FORBES. You and *I*, Max.

GOODMAN. You and I. You and me, whatever. . . . We couldn't do that. . . . It'd be like . . . like . . . Black without Decker.

FORBES. I would have prefered Fortnum without Mason.

GOODMAN. We're a team — Max Goodman and Nigel Forbes.

FORBES. *Forbes* and Goodman.

GOODMAN. Right! You take top billing, Nije, and I wouldn't have it any other way. I couldn't do it without you. There, I've admitted it at last. I may come up with the ideas — but without you . . . ? You channel them — point me in the right direction. Well, start pointing me, Nije . . . start motivating!

FORBES. We-ll . . . if we *are* to have another go at it . . .

GOODMAN. Of course we are. We must.

FORBES. We would have to start from square one. A completely new plot.

GOODMAN. Agreed! And we'll sweat over it, we'll burn

the midnight oil . . . and we'll do as we always do—run it through, act it out, until we're sure that every last detail works. Now—where to start—a nice juicy murder—something bizarre and outrageous—and yet, so real it would stand up in a court of law. That's *my* speciality . . . something that will keep them on the edge of their seats, with bated breath, until the big, big twist, at the end . . . and that's *your* speciality, Nije!

FORBES. It sounds wonderful, Max—but we don't have a beginning or an end yet. We don't even have a victim. And, as you know, we always start with a victim.

GOODMAN. (*Nods, and starts to pace to and fro. Suddenly he has a thought:*) A de-frocked priest! No, we tried that and it didn't work. (*GOODMAN resumes his pacing. Then gets another idea:*) I've got it! A heart surgeon. It hasn't been done before. He gets the operation wrong. The husband dies—the wife's seeking revenge. . . .

FORBES. But all our sympathy would be with the surgeon! In the best thrillers one must always have a sneaking regard for the murderer. No, what we want is the victim the *audience* would cheerfully strangle. A victim you love to hate!

ANN. (*off-stage*) Nigel! *Nigel! (They both react, and then ANN FORBES Enters, in an angry mood.) Nigel.* You know what *I* want, don't you?

FORBES. Don't tempt me.

GOODMAN. You've run out of gin?

ANN. If that's your idea of wit, no wonder no one buys your plays anymore. I want it back, and I want it now!

FORBES. Want what back?

ANN. The thirty pounds I put on the shelf under the jam pot. Don't deny you took it, you've got that squinty eyed, devious look, the sort you see on 'wanted' posters! Where is it?

FORBES. I haven't got it.

ANN. That won't wash. I KNOW it was you . . .

FORBES. I've spent it.

ANN. Spent it!? How? It was there this morning!

FORBES. That chap from the garage called—while you were in the bath. Demanded what I owed him for those new tyres. If I hadn't paid him he was going to take the tyres back there and then.

GOODMAN. You'd be lost without a car out here.

ANN. Damn you, Nigel Forbes. Damn both of you! I've got to go and face that man in the off-licence today.

FORBES. Well, you do your fair share of the drinking around here.

GOODMAN. MORE than your fair share.

FORBES. Anyway, you have a cheque book of your own . . .

ANN. Husbands are supposed to keep wives. Not that you'd notice around here — I've been paying most of the bills lately. And now, what I've got I intend to keep. The way you two are going, it looks as though I'm going to need it! Money! Now! Twenty pounds will do.

FORBES. I haven't got twenty pounds.

ANN. Then find it!

FORBES. How?

ANN. Make savings! Fire your secretary . . . fire Jill. Oh no, you wouldn't do that, would you? You'd put her before me every time. . . . There's probably something going on between you . . .

FORBES. That's ridiculous.

ANN. Oh, is it? It wasn't ridiculous in "Death Game" was it — that actress with the long legs? Or "Murder me Softly"? Or "Killer's Return"?

GOODMAN. That was a failure.

ANN. Not for him and the leading lady it wasn't. Mind you, that was a long time ago when he could still do it. . . . Now he can't even write a successful play.

GOODMAN. And we're just about to do it again—we're on the brink of something big. . . . Aren't we, Nije?

ANN. Oh, *you're* going to give him a leg up, are you? That depresses me. Now do I get that money or don't I?

FORBES. I haven't bloody well got it.

ANN. Well bloody well get it.

FORBES. How? Where?

ANN. Well, if your friends weren't all paupers you could borrow it.

GOODMAN. Not quite paupers. (*He takes some money from his pocket, and gives it to ANN.*) There's your twenty pounds. (*FORBES and ANN are surprised. Eventually:*)

ANN. Don't run away with the idea that this is a loan. You've been poncing food and drink off us for weeks . . . (*She moves to the door, regards them, and:*) "On the brink of something big, eh"? If it turns out to be a ravine, I'd throw yourselves in! (*She Exits. A long moment, then:*)

FORBES. *That's* who we should be planning to kill. (*He moves across to pour himself a drink.*) For the umpteenth time in our long relationship, Max, I apologise for my cow of a wife.

GOODMAN. Don't apologise. Why apologise? Don't you see? You said it. *She's* it! (*FORBES regards GOODMAN with a puzzled frown.*) Ann. The perfect victim. "A sneaking regard for the murderer"—when we kill Ann, the audience will give us a standing ovation!

FORBES. When we kill Ann?

GOODMAN. In the play, Nije, in the play—I can see it shaping up now—there's this alcoholic harridan with her hand on the purse strings. . . . Married to this man. . . .

FORBES. . . . A man she trapped into marriage. Yes,

I see him as tall, handsome, mature . . .

GOODMAN. That's you.

FORBES. And virile. Yes, definately virile. (*then:*) No, out of the question.

GOODMAN. Why?

FORBES. The husband would be the first suspect.

GOODMAN. But we'll give him a cast iron alibi.

FORBES. How?

GOODMAN. We-ll . . . Well, he has to be miles away when the murder actually happens — with witnesses to prove it.

FORBES. There's the weakness. If he's miles away, how does he do it?

GOODMAN. Well, er . . . He doesn't do it!

FORBES. He doesn't?

GOODMAN. No — because he has a friend — right? A good friend . . .

FORBES. That's you.

GOODMAN. Right. *Right!* And these two friends . . .

FORBES. That's you and I. . . .

GOODMAN. Right. They're partners in some venture. Accountants. No, too dull. Vets? No . . .

FORBES. Writers?

GOODMAN. Of course. You've done it again, Nije. A writing partnership.

FORBES. Mmmm . . . Ira Levin did it in "Deathtrap."

GOODMAN. *They* were homosexuals. Now as far as *we're* concerned . . . for homosexual read 'buddies' . . . camaraderie.

FORBES. It's terribly close to "Strangers on a Train."

GOODMAN. They *swapped* murders. We're not swapping. . . . I'm just doing your murder for you.

FORBES. You *are* right, Max. It *is* taking shape.

GOODMAN. Taking shape, it's terrific — we're really cooking again, Nije. Now — why do I agree to commit your murder?

(*A long pause — then:*)

FORBES. Their writing partnership hasn't been working?

GOODMAN. Right! *Right!* In fact, it's falling apart, and to make matters worse, they're desperate for money — particularly the good friend — that's me. And the nice guy — that's you again is too . . . Is too . . .

FORBES. Noble?

GOODMAN. Exactly! He's too noble to reveal to his partner the real reason. To tell of the sleepless nights, his wife's constant nagging . . .

FORBES. Yes! He's far too noble to admit that *she* is the reason for his mental exhaustion. So he invents an excuse — a fiction. . . .

GOODMAN. . . . Something like 'The spark of creativity once between them appears to have died.'

FORBES. That's a rather good line, Max — make a note of it . . . (*GOODMAN nods, moves to his desk, and writes on a sheet of paper.*) So — the husband is close to breaking up their working relationship . . .

GOODMAN. But his friend won't hear of it.

FORBES. And he's ready to help.

GOODMAN. Ready to do anything. Anything at all.

FORBES. So together — they come up with this plan to murder the wife. What shall we call her?

GOODMAN. Why not 'Ann'? It's short, and easy to type.

FORBES. All right, for the moment, we'll call her Ann. Now, the question is — how do they do it?

GOODMAN. Slow poison?

FORBES. Tempting—especially if we're calling her Ann. By the way, where did you get twenty pounds?

GOODMAN. You know what a camera buff I am?

FORBES. Yes.

GOODMAN. Well, now I'm not.

FORBES. You sold your camera . . . ? Oh, Max . . .

GOODMAN. They'll be other cameras. Once we've written this new play. And we're nearly there—we have a victim—now all we need is a murder method . . .

(*JILL Enters carrying a tray of coffee.*)

JILL. Coffee up!

GOODMAN. Thanks, Jill . . .

(*JILL puts the tray on the antique chest, then moves away to FORBES' desk.*)

FORBES. I always like a good strangulation.

GOODMAN. Yes—it goes on as long as you want it to—if the play's running short, a good director can pick up some time there.

FORBES. And not only that, it's sort of sexy too . . . flexing a stocking between one's hands . . .

GOODMAN. And you know how actors love props.

JILL. (*Has picked up a card from FORBES' desk, and waited. She now tries to attract attention:*) Hmm . . . Hmm . . .

FORBES. But one does lose the marvellous shock effect of blood suddenly splashed across the stage.

GOODMAN. But you do get the choking cries.

JILL. Excuse me . . .

FORBES. They seem to expect violence these days. Television has ruined them. *Excuse me.*

FORBES. Yes, what is it?

JILL. I'll be going into town later. This card from the optician's has been lying here for more than a week. Your spare pair of glasses have been repaired. Do you want me to pick them up?

FORBES. Yes, yes, collect them . . . (*He turns back to GOODMAN.*) Now about this murder method.

JILL. They'll be something to pay. Twenty five pounds, perhaps thirty . . .

FORBES. Oh, well, er . . . I'll pick them up myself. Next week. Now, Max. . . . (*JILL clears her throat to denote that she has not finished. FORBES turns on her.*) Are you still here?

JILL. I'm sorry, but while we're on about money — I hate to bring this up, but . . . well, I haven't been paid for last month.

FORBES. If you hate to bring it up, why did you?

GOODMAN. Oh, come on, Nije — that's unfair!

JILL. I'm not asking for the money.

FORBES. Why not? Everybody else is!

JILL. I'm just pointing out that I have to eat too. Come the end of the month I'll have to start looking elsewhere. It's not that I *want* to leave — no — I've loved working for you, I really have . . . but . . . well . . . it's just that . . . You must understand?

FORBES. Oh, yes — we understand all right.

GOODMAN. Nije! (*He moves round to face JILL.*) Sure we understand — but it may not come to that, Jill. We're onto something — all we have to do is work out the details, and then . . . get at it.

JILL. I hope so . . . And I wish you luck . . . (*She moves to the door, opens it, then pauses and looks back!*)

Why don't you use a gun? (*GOODMAN reacts.*) For the murder you're planning. I don't think I've typed in a gun since I started working for you. (*She Exits, and closes the door behind herself.*)

GOODMAN. You shouldn't bully her like that, Nije. She's a terrific girl — good looking too. Attractive.

FORBES. Hmm, yes — I suppose so. *Why not a gun?*

GOODMAN. There's the noise factor. It'll wake up the maid, the butler . . . Although I suppose it could be a household without servants?

FORBES. A thriller? Without servants? And who would answer the ringing phone as the curtain goes up? Besides, we may need a minor character to carry the humour . . .

GOODMAN. You think so? I thought the two writers would be quite funny guys.

FORBES. Oh, no. One of them has a rapier-like wit. . . . (*FORBES — un-noticed — looks GOODMAN up and down:*) I see the other as . . . rather dull.

(*ANN Enters carrying some mail — which she puts down as follows:*)

ANN. Mail . . . (*She puts down one letter.*) Bills . . . (*She puts down a batch of envelopes.*) Final demands! (*She puts down a bigger batch of envelopes. She moves to Exit, then pauses:*) Just look at the two of you. Has-beens, still scribbling away to try and find the old fire. Well, you won't — it isn't there anymore. Perhaps it never was. You may have to start thinking about getting a proper job! (*She regards them with a mocking gaze as:*) Or perhaps you, Nigel, could put your criminal tendencies to better use? Go out and rob a bank or something? No, whatever you do will always be small time.

Stealing thirty quid from under a jam pot is just about your mark! (*She Exits. A pause, then:*)

GOODMAN. Marvellous! They'll hate her the minute she comes on. Do we have a victim, or do we have a victim! It's terrific. It's wonderful. It's no good.

FORBES. What?

GOODMAN. Motive. Why would you want to kill Ann?

FORBES. You ask me . . . after that?

GOODMAN. That was real life—but we need to do better than that for the theatre. Why *would* you kill Ann?

FORBES. I'm not going to kill her—you are.

GOODMAN. Why would *I* then? Wouldn't I just tell you to divorce her? You've got grounds enough.

FORBES. For the money.

GOODMAN. For twenty quid?

FORBES. For the insurance.

GOODMAN. What insurance?

FORBES. Two hundred thousand pounds upon her death—I took it out during the flush of our first real success.

GOODMAN. The "Murder Plot"?

FORBES. Ah, Max, things were going well then.

GOODMAN. Don't remind me. . . . Two hundred thousand pounds?

FORBES. It would come straight to me of course.

GOODMAN. Now that's a really strong motive. That's the kind of money a man would murder for.

FORBES. Yes, and I could certainly use one hundred thousand pounds right now.

GOODMAN. A hundred? I thought you said it was two hundred thousand pounds.

FORBES. I'd split it with you, wouldn't I? I mean, as you would be doing the actual killing.

GOODMAN. A hundred thousand.

FORBES. Each.

GOODMAN. That *would* get us out of a hole.

FORBES. The pressure would be off us then

GOODMAN. We could take our time about the next play.

FORBES. Refine. Get it right. Just like the old days, Max, before I married Ann.

GOODMAN. Sounds like a wonderful dream.

FORBES. Yes.

GOODMAN. But a pipe dream. It won't work.

FORBES. Eh?

GOODMAN. The insurance, Nije. The motive. . . . It would point the finger straight at you!

FORBES. You're right. I thought for a moment we were on to another "Death Has No Exit". *That* gave us a lot of early problems too.

GOODMAN. Yes, but making the vicar's wife a karate expert won't help us here!

FORBES. Hmmm. . . . (*FORBES has moved to his desk. He has sat down and idly opened and glanced through his mail. He has put on his heavy reading glasses.*) I remember you buying that camera, Max — how excited you were . . .

GOODMAN. Get this right and there'll be a dozen cameras!

FORBES. Yes, and by God, Max, we've got to make this play work somehow. We've got to!

GOODMAN. I've been thinking about it. Suppose the husband has a secret mistress? (*FORBES gives GOOD-MAN a hard look.*) O.K. O.K. No secret mistress. But you see where I'm leading? We have to create another suspect. *Invent* one.

FORBES. (*scanning a letter*) An anonymous letter containing a veiled threat to kill my wife.

GOODMAN. Oh, great, Nije, you've done it again! Where do they come from?

FORBES. (*examining the envelope*) London South West Ten. . . . That's Fulham, isn't it? Or is it Chelsea?

GOODMAN. What? You mean an actual letter?

FORBES. An actual letter, postmarked yesterday afternoon. Obviously from some crank — listen to this . . . (*reads*) "Dear Mr. Playwright, I suppose you think you're brilliant. . . ."

GOODMAN. Well, so far so good . . .

FORBES. ". . . creating a wonderfully worked-out hanging on stage. . . ."

GOODMAN. He's talking about "Death Game". That was six years ago . . . and anyway the hanging was *my* idea, why is he writing to you?

FORBES. Because you have no wife. It continues . . . ". . . . as a result of seeing this perverted play presented under the guise of entertainment. . . ."

GOODMAN. It's a critic — got to be a critic!

FORBES. ". . . . as a result, my dear wife was so influenced as to emulate the sick example you set in such detail and now lies dead, leaving me bereft and bitter. . . . But let me assure you that one day soon you will come to know the shock of bereavement . . ." It's ending on a brighter note. ". . . and be left a sad and lonely widower as I am."

GOODMAN. How's it signed? "A Well-wisher"?

FORBES. No signature. Typewritten. (*He removes his glasses, and hands the letter to GOODMAN*) It's the vicar's wife all over again — the breakthrough. Oh, I know we've had crank notes in the past. . . . But never one that actually mentioned my wife . . .

GOODMAN. But, as you said, it's only a *veiled* threat.

FORBES. That's its strength, don't you see? Its ambiguity. . . . Of course you and I know he has no intention of actually doing anything.

GOODMAN. But if Ann *were* to be murdered . . .

FORBES. And I. . . .

GOODMAN. Suspect Number One . . .

FORBES. Had an absolutely cast-iron alibi . . .

GOODMAN. They'd have to look elsewhere. . . .

FORBES. This letter would become enormously significant then. It would be their only clue.

(*A pause. They regard each other.*)

GOODMAN. I like it. You know why I like it? It isn't contrived. It has a neat simplicity about it. This crank never actually says he *is* going to kill your wife . . .

FORBES. But the hint is there.

GOODMAN. It's the kind of clue you or I might have written.

FORBES. Just enough to muddy the waters.

GOODMAN. Cast a doubt.

(*FORBES regards the letter he now holds, then carefully puts it away in his desk, as:*)

FORBES. This suddenly makes everything possible.

GOODMAN. Now it's just a question of mechanics — and dreaming up exactly the right plot.

FORBES. I'm not sure that it's *dreaming,* Max. More a question of choosing . . .

GOODMAN. What do you mean?

FORBES. I mean originality might be dangerous — we want something that's come under close scrutiny and passed muster. . . . Something proven.

GOODMAN. Eh?

FORBES. A classic concept.

GOODMAN. You're not suggesting. . . . ? You don't mean *steal*? Plagiarize?

FORBES. Let's be realistic, Max, we thought our last play was superbly original, and look what happened to that. No, we have to go back to the grass roots for this one — to the classic murder plays.

GOODMAN. But in the classic plays, the murderer always gets caught.

FORBES. Because the author wanted him caught. Our play will have a happy ending. For the murderer. (*He wanders over to the bookshelves, and runs his hand over a section.*) I think we can eliminate all the Christie plays . . . Much as I admire the old duck, they do lean rather heavily upon exactitudes of time, esoteric clues, and policemen on skis. . . .

GOODMAN. "Night Must Fall"?

FORBES. (*shudders*) The idea of touting that head around in a hat-box is utterly repellent. What about "Bleuth"?

GOODMAN. Brilliant, craftsmanslike job . . .

FORBES. I agree . . . But all that dressing up . . . ! (*He takes a book from the shelves*) "Dial M For Murder"!

GOODMAN. I hated that play.

FORBES. Why on earth should you? It's in constant production — made a fortune.

GOODMAN. That's why I hate it . . .

FORBES. Ah, Max, but now is not the time for professional jealousies . . . now is the time to learn from the best — and, in my opinion, Frederick Knott *is* one of the best. "Dial M For Murder" — superbly constructed, exciting denouement, big film sales — what more could one ask? Yes, "Dial M". That's the one.

GOODMAN. There's another reason I'm against that play.

FORBES. Oh?

GOODMAN. Under our present construction, I'm the murderer — right?

FORBES. I wouldn't have cast it any other way.

GOODMAN. Well — in "Dial M" it's the murderer who gets killed!

FORBES. Ah, but when Freddy Knott wrote "Dial M" it suited his purpose to have the murder go wrong. *Ours* is going to go right.

GOODMAN. How?

FORBES. Well . . . How many times have you seen the play?

GOODMAN. Half a dozen at least.

FORBES. I thought you hated it.

GOODMAN. I'm a masochist.

FORBES. All right. Chief plotter — that's me — blackmails potential murderer — that's you — into killing Chief plotter's wife. . . . Is my recollection correct?

GOODMAN. So far.

FORBES. Now the murder — and this is Freddy Knotts master stroke — killer waits here in the shadows — phone rings — wife enters to answer it — killer pounces.

GOODMAN. And she stabs him dead.

FORBES. That's *his* version — we're going to fix that. Now — *our* version is — killer waits — phone rings — wife in — killer pounces — *wife* dead. Does that suit you better?

GOODMAN. It's easy to say — how are we going to achieve it?

FORBES. We are going to improve upon Freddy Knotts' construction. What was the weakness of "Dial M For Murder"?

GOODMAN. It only ran five years?

FORBES. The murder method. Strangling — thus putting killer and victim in close proximity — and, as if that wasn't enough — leaving a convenient pair of scissors on the desk for her to stab him with.

GOODMAN. Got you! We're going to move the desk.

FORBES. No, we are not going to move the desk.

GOODMAN. Move the scissors?

FORBES. No, you are going to use a gun. And fire from over there, by the french windows.

GOODMAN. I like it. I like it. I don't like it.

FORBES. Why not?

GOODMAN. We're two writers — O.K.?

FORBES. Yes.

GOODMAN. And I'm going to kill your wife for you.

FORBES. Yes.

GOODMAN. With a gun.

FORBES. Yes.

GOODMAN. So where does a *writer* get a gun from?

FORBES. (*pointing towards the ceiling*) From the attic! I got it from my father, and *he* got it from a German Officer. It's illegal, of course, but utterly untraceable to me.

GOODMAN. It's a good job we just *write* crimes.

FORBES. Yes, ironic isn't it? Our only talent is for murder and mayhem and getting away with it until the last page. Just suppose we put all that experience to a more practical use?

GOODMAN. If we did — we'd have to get away with it *beyond* the last page.

FORBES. Oh, I'm sure we could — if we put our minds to it, aren't you?

GOODMAN. I wouldn't be *that* confident. Our detectives are always so bloody brilliant.

FORBES. Only because we write them that way.

GOODMAN. Anyway, it's all hypothetical — we're not doing it for real, are we?

(*A pause. Then:*)

FORBES. I'll get the gun. It may inspire us.

(*FORBES Exits. GOODMAN, alone on stage, moves about, obviously turning the plot over in his mind. He becomes the killer — makes a gun with his fingers — and 'fires' at the door:*)

GOODMAN. Bang! Bang!

(*At this precise moment ANN Enters, to stand staring at GOODMAN and his 'gun'. They regard each other for a long moment.*)

ANN. Cowboys and bloody indians at your age! (*She moves to get herself a drink.*)
GOODMAN. I'm working out our new play. We're off and running again. A terrific idea. Going to put us back on top—just like the old days.
ANN. Did you ever hear back from that American company?

(*GOODMAN's eager optimism fades a bit, he hesitates, then, putting on a brave face:*)

GOODMAN. Well, it . . . it takes time for the stuff to get out there. And . . . and a big company like that, lot of people have to read it first. I'll bet it's on the Managing Director's desk right now!
ANN. Or hanging in the men's room!
GOODMAN. That's not fair. All right, we HAVE been going through a bad patch but . . .
ANN. (*interjects*) *Patch*!? If Nelson had worn your 'bad

patch' you wouldn't have seen his feet! It's been years . . .

GOODMAN. You shouldn't go on like this. Nigel needs *encouragement* not . . .

ANN. (*interjects*) What Nigel needs is a brain transplant. Or possibly just a new partner would do.

GOODMAN. Why did you say that?

ANN. He's mooted the idea. Hasn't he mentioned it to you?

GOODMAN. Only in passing, he wasn't thinking straight.

ANN. I think it's the straightest thinking he's done in years. He did write a few decent plays before he met you, you know? Yes, if he were solo again it might give him new purpose. In any event it would be one less mouth to feed around here!

(*As ANN moves to Exit:*)

GOODMAN. Our partnership isn't going to break up. I won't let that happen, d'you hear!? It's going to stay as it is . . . the two of us . . . (*ANN Exits. GOODMAN looks deflated as:*) Whatever it takes. Whatever.

(*FORBES Enters, carrying a small box, and looking puzzled.*)

FORBES. What on earth did she mean?

GOODMAN. Who?

FORBES. Ann. She said General Custer was waiting for me.

GOODMAN. Oh, she's half cut as usual. Come on, Nije, let's get on with the play.

FORBES. The play? Oh, yes, the play. (*FORBES opens*

*the box and takes out a gun and places it on the desk.
GOODMAN regards it with some awe.)*

GOODMAN. A real gun.

FORBES. With real ammunition. (*FORBES produces
box of ammunition and places that on desk, too. GOOD-
MAN picks up the gun to examine it.*) Max, I've been
thinking—it would be a dreadful thing to end our
relationship.

GOODMAN. I couldn't agree more.

FORBES. But we really have only one alternative. That
is to set this new play here, in this house . . .

GOODMAN. Got no objection to that—make the de-
signer's job easier . . .

FORBES. And do it for real.

GOODMAN. Real? Sorry, I don't follow you . . .

FORBES. I mean, do it. Murder Ann.

GOODMAN. You can't be serious?

FORBES. Deadly serious. This is the best idea you have
had in years, Max, and I KNOW it will work.

GOODMAN. Come on, Nije . . . you can't
mean . . . ? That you and I . . . ? That we
should . . . ?

FORBES. Yes, that's exactly what I am suggesting. Half
an hour ago I too would have considered it madness, but
your brilliant, incisive mind has suddenly made it en-
tirely possible.

GOODMAN. Murder Ann?

FORBES. Come now, it WAS your idea. You pointed
out what a perfect victim she is.

GOODMAN. Yes, but for the play . . . I mean to actually do it . . . to murder Ann . . . ?

FORBES. Let's approach it as we do all our plots. The
'fors' and "againsts" For . . . She is a drunken shrew
we would be well rid of. What money she does have

would come to me. And two hundred thousand pounds insurance. A return to solvency for both of us. The againsts? You tell me, Max.

GOODMAN. Well. . . . Well, we might not get away with it!

FORBES. Fail? Us? If you think that, Max—that the team of Forbes and Goodman is not capable of producing a plot without a single error . . . Well—perhaps it *is* time for the parting of the ways.

GOODMAN. I didn't mean that.

FORBES. Then what did you mean? (*then:*) It's time for a decision, Max.

GOODMAN. Is that policy paid up to date?

FORBES. Absolutely. It's the one thing I haven't let fall by the way side.

GOODMAN. Two hundred thousand pounds?

FORBES. Split two ways.

GOODMAN. One hundred thousand each. It's a lot of loot.

FORBES. Our salvation.

GOODMAN. Yes. . . . And she did call me a ponce. (*GOODMAN suddenly hurries over to his typewriter and starts to type.*)

FORBES. Max, what are you doing?

GOODMAN. Got to get it down while it's still fresh.

FORBES. No, Max, I don't think we will be committing this one to paper, will we? We'll tape it. (*FORBES draws the paper from the typewriter, and moves away, tearing it up, and throwing it into the waste basket. He crosses to the tape recorder. We hear the clicks as he operates the buttons.*) We'll record, play back, assimilate . . . And then—erase. It's nice to be back in harness again—working together on something we *both* believe in.

GOODMAN. The thought of killing Ann . . .

FORBES. Max! Get a grip on yourself!

GOODMAN. No . . . No, I was just going to say . . . It makes me feel *alive* again!

THE CURTAIN FALLS

SCENE 2.

THE CURTAIN RISES ON: NIGEL FORBES' Study. Some time later.
As in the opening of Scene One, the heavy drapes at the french windows are drawn, and the set is dark.
GOODMAN can just be seen in the shadows near the french windows.
The telephone is ringing. After a few moments, the door opens and ANN enters.
GOODMAN brings up his hand, making his fingers a gun as he 'aims' at the door and ANN.
ANN switches on the light and reacts as she sees GOODMAN 'aiming' at her.

ANN. For God's sake, you're not at it again! Playing around in the dark . . . why the hell don't you answer the phone? (*As she speaks, she picks up the phone.*)

GOODMAN. It's the engineers.

ANN. Hello? What? Well, of course it's working—how do you think I'm talking to you, by telepathy! (*ANN slams the phone down again.*) Testing the line!

GOODMAN. That was for me . . .

ANN. A last fling before they cut it off!?

GOODMAN. I was checking something out. *For the new play.*

ANN. I think you're *kinky*. Sitting here in the dark—poking your fingers at me . . .

GOODMAN. They're not fingers, they're a gun!

ANN. Cowboys and indians!

GOODMAN. *Research*!

ANN. Someone should research YOU! Not that they'd find much — but it might make the basis of a play — autobiographical — "One Fell Into The Cuckoo's Nest"! (*ANN moves to Exit, but:*)

GOODMAN. Thank you, Ann.

ANN. For what!?

GOODMAN. Making it easy for me.

ANN. (*staring at him, then, shaking her head.*) Kinky.

(*ANN Exits. GOODMAN hurries over to switch off the light again, then moves to his 'killing position', aims his 'gun' and:*)

GOODMAN. Ring, ring. Ring, ring. (*FORBES Enters and puts on the lights.*), then GOODMAN. Now you're doing it. Now you're doing it.

FORBES. Doing what?

GOODMAN. Putting on the lights. So did Ann a moment ago as I killed her.

FORBES. (*alarmed, looking for the body*) Killed her!? You fool! It's much too soon . . .

GOODMAN. (*over-rides*) As I *practised* killing her. And she put on the light.

FORBES. Well, it's the natural thing to do.

GOODMAN. But if she turns on the light — she'll see me — she may duck — even throw something . . .

FORBES. Then she won't put on the light. We'll replace the bulb with a dud one.

GOODMAN. Great. You know, Nije, just now, as I pointed my gun at her I felt . . . good. Elated . . . (*then*) She'll go straight to the desk lamp and put that on!

FORBES. She's not supposed to get as far as the desk.

GOODMAN. But she might.

FORBES. All right, we'll put a dud bulb in there too.

GOODMAN. TWO dud bulbs? Any copper worth his salt will be onto that in a flash.

FORBES. I'll replace them next morning before I call the police. Right?

GOODMAN. Right. RIGHT!

FORBES. But if all goes to plan she will not get to the desk lamp — because she will be dead — because you will shoot her as she opens the door and stands silhouetted — a perfect target. Your killing position will be over there, by the french windows. The phone rings — she enters . . .

GOODMAN. She mustn't be allowed to answer the phone . . .

FORBES. Why not?

GOODMAN. Detail, Nije, detail. She mustn't be allowed to answer the phone because we can't guarantee it will be you on the other end.

FORBES. Yes, I see.

GOODMAN. It's agony to fail at the box-office, Nije — but to fail at the Old Bailey would be fatal . . .

FORBES. Let's run it through from the top again. I'll be staying at my club in town — thus establishing a cast-iron alibi.

GOODMAN. Ann will be in the drawing room.

FORBES. With her gin and television. Then — at precisely nine fifteen I will call the business number which rings here — and Ann will have to come in to answer it.

GOODMAN. I'll already be in the room . . . Having entered through the french windows.

FORBES. Which I will make sure are unlocked. So — Ann enters — you get your silhouette.

GOODMAN. And . . . "bang-bang".

(*FORBES and GOODMAN stare at each other, and GOODMAN gives a big smile.*)

GOODMAN. It's going to work, Nije . . .
FORBES. Of course it's going to work . . .
GOODMAN. Now. . . .

(*GOODMAN stands, moves to the french windows, and surveys the room. He points to where the body will lie:*)

GOODMAN. After I've done it I mustn't go near the body—I can't risk the tiniest splash of blood.
FORBES. No—you leave the house the way you came in, and—next morning—I return, discover the body, call the police and . . .
GOODMAN. Suppose you don't discover the body?
FORBES. Max—I shall make a definite point of doing so.
GOODMAN. No, no, suppose somebody beats you to it?
FORBES. Who for example?
GOODMAN. I don't know—the shooting is going to make a noise.
FORBES. The curtains will muffle it, and our nearest neighbour is miles away.
GOODMAN. You might have a burglar.
FORBES. I would welcome a burglar. I would welcome any unexpected visitor as just another suspect. Let's continue . . . The gun?
GOODMAN. Untraceable to you. He brought it with him. I leave it on the floor.
FORBES. Yes—but how do we give the crank some substance . . .
GOODMAN. Mmmm . . . I've got it. His letter re-

ferred to the hanging in "Death Game"—Before the phone rings I take *our* copy of the play, and tear it up. . . .

FORBES. *Before* the phone rings. . . .? That's another hole to plug. Suppose the phone rang ahead of time, and Ann came in to answer it . . . ?

GOODMAN. . . . . And walked in on me while I was still setting up—before I was ready. O.K. first thing I do is take the phone off the hook. . . .

FORBES. . . . . And replace it at nine fifteen . . .

GOODMAN. Right. I take up my position, and . . . it's going to work, Nije. We've overlooked nothing. Yes we have!

FORBES. What?

GOODMAN. If both bulbs are dud—I'll be in the dark. I won't be able to see a thing!

FORBES. *Max. . . .* (*He opens a drawer in his desk and takes out the torch.*)

GOODMAN. A torch! (*He crosses and takes it.*) It's like we always say—come to a complex problem, and invariably you can solve it in the simplest way . . .

FORBES. Now where were we?

GOODMAN. I'd just replaced the phone . . .

FORBES. Correct. At nine fifteen precisely, I call this number—the phone rings. . . .

(*FORBES and GOODMAN are both startled as the phone does start to RING. FORBES answers it.*)

FORBES. Hello? Ah, yes, Superintendent, this is he. You have a man on his way? Splendid! Yes, I look forward to meeting him. Goodbye. (*He replaces the phone and turns to GOODMAN.*) The police about the crank letter. I rang earlier this morning. There'll be a man here anytime, but there should be time for one last run through to check fine details. You get by the curtains, Max. . . (*FORBES crosses to switch off the light as he speaks. GOODMAN stands by the french windows, and once again the set is in darkness.*) All right. Make your entrance.

(*GOODMAN steps further into the room, and—immediately—collides with the fridge.*)

GOODMAN. Damn! I forgot the torch!

(*On the collision the door of the fridge has swung open, and the light from within illuminates the room.*)

FORBES. Stay where you are! Don't move! (*He crosses to the fridge and swings the door to and fro to give a lighting effect.*) Compliments of Frederick Knott. "Wait Until Dark."
GOODMAN. But we're not doing that play! Besides I'll have the torch!

(*FORBES closes the fridge, and moves to the french windows. He draws the curtains, and sunlight beams through.*)

FORBES. It's a weak link, Max. You still might bump into the fridge — and then what? The door opens — light floods out — Ann sees you. . . .
GOODMAN. Well, what do we do about it?
FORBES. As soon as you come in, you pull the plug on the fridge.
GOODMAN. But who'll put it back? I won't have time.
FORBES. I'll put it back the next morning.

GOODMAN. It's getting awfully complicated—dud bulbs—fridges—unhooking phones—tearing up plays . . . I hope I'll have enough time left to do the actual murder! By the time I've finished, my fishing trip will be more than an alibi, it'll be a convalescence.

FORBES. Ah, yes—your alibi. I'm glad you reminded me.

GOODMAN. Well, it may not be the best I've ever written but it'll do . . .

FORBES. But will it hold up? Alone on a desolate stretch of river, fishing through the night until dawn.

GOODMAN. Nobody can prove otherwise, and it has a ring of truth. Everybody knows I go fishing. And I know that area. You can go a whole weekend and never meet a soul.

FORBES. On the other hand, the lack of witnesses means that you cannot prove you were there.

GOODMAN. Nije, at the time of the murder, I'd like to be on Concorde, mid-Atlantic, accompanied by a nun's convention, but somebody has to be here to actually do it!

FORBES. But with me in the clear, we can't have you becoming a suspect—it wouldn't be fair.

GOODMAN. Why should I become a suspect? I've no reason to murder Ann.

FORBES. Well—you don't exactly like her.

GOODMAN. Now that is a bit of an understatement. I hate the bitch!

FORBES. Exactly—and suppose that were to come out?

GOODMAN. Mmmm. I see what you mean.

FORBES. It's a point we'll have to cover—for your sake. But how? (*He paces, in thought, then:*) Detective Inspector Berry!

GOODMAN. Who's he?

FORBES. The policeman who will be arriving here at any moment. Max, we've created enough policemen to know that they form first, immediate, and lasting impressions. There mustn't be the slightest hint that you hate her.

GOODMAN. What are you driving at?

FORBES. You and Ann. If we can contrive that the two of you are seen together—without acrimony, without hate—with a rapport even . . .

GOODMAN. A rapport? Me and Ann . . . ?

FORBES. Just for Inspector Berry's benefit. A kind word, a gesture of affection . . .

GOODMAN. Affection! Ann'll think I've gone round the bend . . . or I'm trying to get my twenty quid back! (*The doorbell RINGS.*)

FORBES. That's probably him now! Max, if you can contrive to send him away with the impression that there *might* be a little more between you and Ann. . . .

GOODMAN. I'll try, but it won't be easy.

FORBES. You're talking to a man who has endured her for fifteen years.

JILL. (*OFF*) This way, Inspector. . . .

FORBES. "Enter a detective"—let me 'carry' this scene. Let me do the talking.

(*The door opens, and JILL Enters.*)

JILL. There's a detective. . . .

FORBES. . . . Inspector Berry? Yes, please show him in.

(*DETECTIVE INSPECTOR RAYMOND BERRY Enters. He is perhaps thirty five years of age, or more. Tall, and rather thin, with a walrus moustache that adds to his general, mournful look. He carries a briefcase.)*

BERRY. Good morning, sir . . . Detective Inspector Berry . . .

FORBES. Good morning, Inspector, and I am . . .

BERRY. Oh, I know who you are, sir . . . And you too, sir. Nigel Forbes . . . And Max Goodman. Neither of you needs any introduction.

FORBES. I had no idea we were so notorious . . .

BERRY. Oh, famous, sir, we look upon you as our local celebrities (*He surveys the room.*) Just as I imagined it. Typewriters, shelves full of scripts, drinks at hand, a smattering of antiques . . . and, of course french windows. I knew you'd have french windows. My goodness, you'd be lost without them, wouldn't you? (*FORBES and GOODMAN are a bit taken aback, but, before they can comment:*) Now then, sir . . . I understand it's a matter of a threatening letter?

FORBES. Well, not exactly threatening . . . In fact, on reflection, I feel rather embarrassed troubling you with it.

BERRY. No trouble, sir, no trouble at all. And you two should know better than most that it's from small beginnings that a major crime can blossom. . . . (*FORBES and GOODMAN exchange uncomfortable looks, then:*) May I see the letter, sir?

FORBES. Yes, indeed. . . . (*He puts on his glasses, moves to the desk to search for, and find, the letter. As he does so BERRY picks up his case, and takes out a clear plastic folder. He holds it open so FORBES can drop in the letter.*) There we are, Inspector. Can I offer you a drink?

BERRY. Thank you, sir—a lager if you don't mind . . .

FORBES. Max? (*He moves to the drinks tray, followed by GOODMAN. They pour drinks for themselves, and a lager—taken from the fridge—for BERRY. BERRY puts on his heavy framed reading glasses, and studies the letter, inside the clear plastic folder. FORBES moves back to BERRY, and hands him the glass of lager.*) You can see for yourself, it's obviously from some crank . . .

BERRY. (*taking the lager*) Thank you, sir . . .

GOODMAN. But you never know—better to be safe than sorry, Nije . . .

BERRY. I echo those sentiments, sir. Can see what you mean though—it's cranky enough, but there *is* a hint of threat to your good lady, and perhaps even to yourself. I don't really have to ask *you*, sir, if you kept the envelope?

FORBES. Yes, of course . . . it's here . . . (*He delves into the desk, produces the envelope, and—as BERRY again profers the open clear plastic folder—drops it in with the letter. BERRY is eyeing the typewriter on FORBES' desk. Now:*)

BERRY. And this is where it was written?

FORBES. (*reacting horrified*) No, no, *I* didn't write it. How could you possibly think that I. . . .

BERRY. Not the letter, sir. "Crazy Kill" Of all your plays it's my favourite.

GOODMAN. Oh, you've seen all our plays, have you?

BERRY. Seen or read every one of them. But I've told you that before . . . About three years ago. (*FORBES and GOODMAN react, and exchange a look. BERRY smiles:*) Aha, that's intrigued you, hasn't it? Wondering where we've met before? (*He removes, and puts his spectacles onto FORBES' desk. He picks up his lager, and takes a drink. Then he puts the glass down onto the desk. Then—suddenly—he clutches his throat, and emits a terrifying cry.*) My God, the drink. The drink was poisoned. . . . (*He staggers, and falls to the floor. He rolls onto his back, and lies spreadeagled, his eyes staring glassily. FORBES and GOODMAN are transfixed. They stare, unmoving, at BERRY on the floor. Then, slowly, and together, they rise, and move towards him. As they bend over, and look down on him, BERRY suddenly sits up.*) "Crazy Kill" Act two, scene three, where the villain gets his come-uppance . . . (*He gets to his feet.*) Yes, I've had the honour of appearing in several of your plays, sir. That's where we met — The Home Counties, Thames Division Drama Festival. You adjudicated. Of course, I was aged up, and wearing a full beard at the time, but you both congratulated me on my portrayal of Captain Carruthers. Your praises still ring in my ears. You *do* remember, don't you, sir?

FORBES. Oh, yes, the Amateur Dramatics thing . . . Yes, of course we remember, *don't we, Max*?

GOODMAN. Eh? Oh, yes, yes, memorable performance.

BERRY. Thank you, sir, I tried to rise to the quality of the writing.

FORBES. Do sit down, Inspector.

BERRY. (*doing so*) We're doing "Death Has No Exit" this year, sir, and . . . er, as a matter of fact, I have a confession to make.

FORBES. Oh?

BERRY. Yes, sir, when your call came through . . . Well, it shouldn't strictly have been my enquiry — but I pulled a bit of rank, sir, not just to renew our acquaintance, but to ask your advice too.

FORBES. Advice?

BERRY. How to attack the role, sir
FORBES. "Death Has No Exit". . . . ?
BERRY. It's the one with the parrot.
FORBES. Oh, yes — you'll be splendid, Inspector, absolutely splendid as the bumbling Interpol agent. . . .
BERRY. Well, actually, sir — I'm playing the Spanish gardener. This time I wanted to try my hand at something a bit more dynamic. But there'll be time for more of that later, I hope. Now, this letter, sir.
FORBES. Letter?
GOODMAN. (*nudging Forbes*) The threatening letter!
BERRY. A veiled threat.
FORBES. That's exactly the construction we put on it.
BERRY. Well, as you can see for yourself, it's not written on hand-made, silk-pressed paper, with a water mark indicating it was expressly made for one exiled anarchist. No, I'd say it was Basildon Bond. Sold everywhere. . . . The envelope too — postmarked South West Ten — well, that's a big area . . . So, the only clue is the reference to the play.
GOODMAN. Oh?
BERRY. The only play of yours with a hanging on stage is "Death Game" — correct me if I'm wrong.
FORBES. No, no, you're not wrong.
BERRY. And this letter has a note of bitterness about it that suggests immediacy. . . . I mean, few people carry this kind of grudge for any length of time.
GOODMAN. So?
BERRY. Where in the last week or two, has "Death Game" been performed?
GOODMAN. That's good. That's terribly good, Nije, we must remember that.
FORBES. The Isle of Wight.
BERRY. Sir?

FORBES. Just a fortnight ago it had a production in the Isle of Wight.

BERRY. How long did it run, sir?

GOODMAN. Judging by the royalties, about ten minutes!

FORBES. A week, Inspector, just a week.

BERRY. So — we possibly have a man resident in the South West Ten area of London — on holiday two weeks ago with his wife on the Isle of Wight — and now recently bereaved due to her death by hanging.

FORBES. My goodness, Inspector, I am impressed, that has really narrowed it down.

BERRY. If I have any gift for deduction, sir, it doesn't come from the Police College. It comes from Agatha Christie, Francis Durbridge, and from your goodselves.

FORBES & GOODMAN. That's really very flattering. Most kind of you.

BERRY. Crime is my business, sir — and my hobby. Investigating them. Appearing in them. I'm probably the leading expert in this area. I guessed the murderer in your last play — before the second act. I wouldn't be surprised if in your next effort I didn't spot the killer immediately . . . (*GOODMAN reacts, and exchanges a look with an equally perturbed FORBES. BERRY fails to notice.*) By the way, sir, is the earring mandatory?

GOODMAN. Earring?

BERRY. For the Spanish gardener, sir. I honestly don't feel very happy wearing it. You must remember that our audience is predominently C.I.D., and a lot of Vice Squad.

FORBES. It's not essential, Inspector, it comes down to getting under the skin of the part.

BERRY. Quite, sir.

GOODMAN. The letter, Nije . . .

FORBES. Eh?

GOODMAN. We do have other things to do. Another play to write. . . .

BERRY. Oh, I'm taking up your valuable time, and I promised myself I wouldn't. The letter, yes. Well, on the positive side, we can run all recent female deaths by hanging through the computer—and narrow it down even further. That's if he was telling the truth.

FORBES. What do you mean?

BERRY. Cranks are deluded, sir—and sometimes they delude even themselves—oh, this man has a grudge all right, he obviously doesn't like you . . . but he may be cunning enough to have hidden the real reason. I think all we can safely assume, sir, is that your wife may be in some danger.

GOODMAN. That's great!

(*BERRY and FORBES turn to look at GOODMAN.*)

GOODMAN. Great that you've come to that assumption.

FORBES. Perhaps you'd like to meet my wife, Inspector?

BERRY. Oh, yes, a pleasure, sir.

FORBES. Max, would you go and fetch her?

GOODMAN. What?

FORBES. I think it's important, and I'm sure the Inspector would agree, that he meets the whole household —sees what kind of people he may be protecting . . . *how we relate to one another.*

BERRY. Sort of setting the scene—establishing the main protagonists. Like you always do, sir.

GOODMAN. Oh, yes—understand—got you—with you. I'll get her . . . (*He Exits. FORBES regards*

BERRY for a moment, then:)

FORBES. Burning to ask questions, aren't you?

BERRY. Well, as a matter of fact, sir . . .

FORBES. How a writing collaboration works? Does he write the lines, or do I?

BERRY. Let me guess, sir. You attend to the dramatic structure — right?

FORBES. Well, you're very close . . .

BERRY. And Mr. Goodman — all that nervous energy — he's the one who comes up with the wild and wonderfully murderous ideas.

FORBES. "A" for observation, Inspector.

BERRY. Yes, it must take a very special kind of mind to come up with things like "Death Has No Exit."

FORBES. Yes, Max *is* volatile — but sensitive too. . . . And even a little irrational sometimes.

BERRY. And, if you'll forgive me saying so — even a streak of cruelty. The final scene can be very harrowing. You know, when the girl crosses to the cupboard and pulls out the knife?

FORBES. I don't think I've ever met such a devotee. Surely, in your own line of work, you get involved in more dramatic situations than we could ever invent?

BERRY. Not really, sir. It generally all comes down to a matter of routine. Statements, counter statements, files, reports. In all my years on the Force, I've never once found myself in the library of a snowbound vicarage with all the suspects assembled and the villain waiting to break down and confess under my incisive interrogation. Mind you — I never give up hoping. . . .

(*JILL enters to put some writing paper down on FORBES' desk.*)

FORBES. Of course, you've met my secretary, Miss Prentice . . .

BERRY. Indeed, sir. I do envy you your job.

JILL. Oh?

BERRY. Being in at the conception so to speak — and in at the death. Was it Miss Prentice who brought you the letter, sir?

FORBES. No, ironically enough, it was Ann herself.

BERRY. Ahh. We won't have to fingerprint *you* then.

JILL. Fingerprint?

FORBES. The Inspector is helping us with some research, Jill.

JILL. Oh, I see. Well, Inspector. . . . (*She smiles, and Exits.*)

FORBES. Fingerprints!?

BERRY. I'll have to ask everyone who has handled the letter to pop down to the station to be fingerprinted — it's a matter of elimination, you understand, sir?

FORBES. Of course, and Max and I will be happy to oblige. But my wife . . . ? I'd hate to alarm her unnecessarily . . .

BERRY. I understand, sir. Well, we'll just have to be subtle about it. I know it's a bit early in the day — but do you think you could persuade her to have a drink:

FORBES. Yes. I think that might be arranged.

BERRY. Then I'll just smuggle the glass away, and. . . .

(*ANN enters, and walks straight to the drinks tray. As she pours herself a large drink:*)

FORBES. Ann, my dear, I'd like you to meet Detective Inspector Berry.

*(BERRY extends his hand, but ANN is too busy with the
    drink, she merely gestures, as:)*

ANN. That raving lunatic of a partner of yours is up to
something. He's just enquired after my health so many
times, you'd think he was a beneficiary in my will!
FORBES. That's unfair, dear. You know that Max is
very fond of you.
ANN. Since when?

(GOODMAN Enters.)

GOODMAN. Ann, do sit down. I'll get you a drink. Oh,
you've got one. Never mind, sit down anyway. Next to
me.
ANN. Definitely up to something.
BERRY. Mrs. Forbes, I'm a great admirer of your husband's work.
ANN. Oh, so you've seen the toolshed, have you?

*(FORBES and GOODMAN exchange a look, and then
    laugh:)*

FORBES. You see now where we get our funny lines.
GOODMAN. Ann, dear, what will we do without you?
Would. *Would!* What *would* we do without you. . . .
ANN. Certifiable. Do you deal much with dangerous
lunatics, Inspector?
BERRY. No, Mrs. Forbes — usually just mundane old
criminals.
ANN. How exceedingly dull. A bit like your last flop.
FORBES. It was miscast.
GOODMAN. And they had to carry that awful director.
ANN. Well, thank God, they only had to carry him for
three days.

(*BERRY suddenly slaps his thigh.*)

BERRY. By George! This is a day to remember.

(*FORBES, ANN, and GOODMAN, all stare at him.*)

BERRY. Me being here with you *real* theatricals. It's something I won't forget in a hurry.
ANN. You *are* a real policeman, aren't you?
BERRY. Of course, Madam.
ANN. For a moment I thought this was one of their terrible rehearsals.
BERRY. Rehearsals?
ANN. They act everything out—they're always at it. Sometimes the sofa is an acid bath, or a lime pit . . . And I never know when I get up in the morning whether my husband is a High Court Judge, a brilliant amateur sleuth—or just the man who is planning to murder me!

(*FORBES and GOODMAN both reach for their glasses,
    and take a drink, in unison.*)

BERRY. Oh, you run through all your crimes, do you, sir?
ANN. Run them through? They *commit* them! (*ANN is moving to Exit now—as JILL Enters.*) Don't believe me—ask her! There are times when I think she knows more about what's going on here than I do! (*She Exits, leaving—for a moment—an embarrassed silence.*)
JILL. I wondered if the Inspector would like some coffee?
BERRY. Well, as a matter of fact. . . .
FORBES. I think not, Jill—the Inspector has important work to deal with—and so do we.
JILL. All right. Nice meeting you, Inspector.

(JILL Exits. BERRY moves to FORBES' desk to collect together his things. FORBES picks up ANN'S used glass, using a handkerchief, and crosses to BERRY. BERRY takes from his case a plastic bag, and FORBES drops the glass into it. BERRY puts it into his case, with the folder containing the letter and envelope.)

BERRY. This letter, sir. . . . What are we going to do about it?

FORBES. I feel that just having told you is sufficient.

BERRY. It's up to me then — to put two or three of my best men watching the house day and night.

FORBES/GOODMAN. (*alarmed*) What?!

BERRY. That's what I'd do if I had the unlimited resources of a policeman on the telly. The fact is, though — we're seriously understaffed.

FORBES. I think policemen lurking in the shrubbery might frighten my wife more than the crank.

BERRY. Take your point, sir. What I *will* do is subject this letter to closer examination, try and run the writer to earth — and tell George to keep an eye out.

FORBES. George?

BERRY. Constable Kingham. Your house is on his patch. . . . He patrols past this house most mornings. . . .

FORBES. Only mornings?

BERRY. I suppose I *could* change his route, have him or his relief double back here every night too.

FORBES. I wouldn't hear of it. In fact, I would be most annoyed—*most annoyed*—if the obviously over-stretched resources of the police force were diverted in any way just for the sake of a . . . a stupid crank. It would make him altogether too important.

GOODMAN. Absolutely.

FORBES. And I would not like that, I would not like it at all.

GOODMAN. Absolutely not!

BERRY. It's very good of you to see it that way, sir.

FORBES. It's the only way I *will* see it, Inspector. And I demand you promise there will be no nightly surveilliance on our account.

BERRY. Very well, sir. . . . (*He picks up from FORBES' desk the spectacles he* thinks *are his, and pockets them. He collects his case, and moves for the door.*) Well. . . . (*BERRY hesitates — they regard him and, a little apologetic:*) I hesitate to raise this . . . but . . . well . . . with the joint experience of the theatre AND a police career. . . . Fact of the matter is that *I* have attempted writing too. A thriller of course — and naturally not up to your high standards . . . but . . . if you would be kind enough to take a look . . . perhaps offer a criticism . . . a few words of wisdom . . . ?

FORBES. Delighted, Inspector. Do send it along sometime.

BERRY. Well . . . as a matter of fact . . . I do happen to have a copy with me . . . (*And, with surprising alacrity, he opens his briefcase and takes out an* enormously *thick script. FORBES and GOODMAN regard it with some dismay.*) I'd be most grateful. (*FORBES takes the script and his hands perceptibly dip to the weight of it!*) It's probably a bit overlength.

FORBES. Yes, well, we'll read it with interest, won't we, Max?

GOODMAN. Yes. *But not right away.*

FORBES. We ARE busy at this time — but eventually — I'm sure the Inspector understands . . . . ?

BERRY. I do, sir . . . And . . . in the words of your own Felix Posner in "Murder Has No End" . . . (*He suddenly adopts a crouch, and attitude, of some character and, in a terrible foreign accent:*) "Our paths will cross again. You may not have seen the last of me . . . only . . . the first of me" (*Then, normally*) Good day, gentlemen. . . . (*He Exits. A moment, then FORBES follows him out, to see him off the premises. GOODMAN is left alone. He collects up the glasses, and puts them on the drinks tray. He is very thoughtful. FORBES Enters.*)

GOODMAN. Do you know what? *He* could be the crank letter writer!

FORBES. What? No. . . .

GOODMAN. He knows all our plays. I think he can see right inside our minds — the wheels going round.

FORBES. He doesn't live in Chelsea — or Fulham — or wherever South West Ten is . . .

GOODMAN. He could. Perhaps he's a top Scotland Yard man 'specially brought in to this area . . . (*FORBES stares at GOODMAN.*) In the play, Nije. . . . I'm talking about in the play!

FORBES. Max — we are not writing a play.

GOODMAN. (*A moment, then He registers.*) Oh, no. I'd forgotten . . . I don't know if I'll be able to live with it.

FORBES. But Ann deserves to die.

GOODMAN. Not *that.* The fact that our best plot in years will only have one performance.

(*FORBES moves to his desk, takes out the gun, and starts to load it.*)

GOODMAN. What are you doing?

FORBES. We must do it soon, Max. In fact, we must do it tonight.

GOODMAN. Tonight? Oh, I don't think we should rush into it . . .

FORBES. You heard what Inspector Berry said, "Few people carry such a grudge for any length of time". That's advice straight from the mouth of an expert — and advice we must heed . . .

GOODMAN. Yes, but it's Saturday night, and you always go to your club on. . . . Saturday night. . . .

FORBES. So I do. . . . (*He hands GOODMAN the loaded gun.*) Come on, Max, I'll walk you to your car. (*He puts his arm round GOODMAN's shoulder, and steers him towards the french windows. There's plenty of time for you to prepare, get your fishing togs together, run through your alibi, and then put your feet up for a while . . . Relax. . . . (FORBES and GOODMAN Exit through the french windows. A pause. Then HEAR:*)

ANN. (*off*) Nigel? What did that policeman . . . ?

(*ANN Enters, and registers the study is empty. ANN looks around, and moves across to the drinks tray. She picks up a bottle, tests it is a full one, and pours a drink.*)

ANN. Nigel Forbes, you *are* up to something. Aided and abetted by Max-bloody-Goodman! (*ANN'S speech betrays the fact that she is a little drunk. She moves to GOODMAN'S desk — and looks at some of the papers there — finds nothing — and crosses to FORBES' desk. She rifles through the papers, then turns to look at the tape recorder. ANN moves to it — pushing this and that button. Finally:*)

FORBES' VOICE. At precisely nine fifteen I will call the business number which rings here. And Ann will have to come in and answer it.

GOODMAN'S VOICE. I'll already be in the room, having entered through the french windows.

FORBES' VOICE. Which I will make sure are un-locked. . . . So Ann enters—you get your silhou-ette. . . .

THE CURTAIN FALLS

SCENE 3

*THE CURTAIN RISES ON: NIGEL FORBES' Study.
    It is Saturday night.
The set is empty, the heavy drapes at the french windows
    are drawn. The room is as dark as theatrical licence
    will allow.
A moment, then we HEAR the french windows open.
    GOODMAN enters. He is dressed for an all night
    fishing trip. Anorak, khaki trousers, scarf, etc. He
    wears gloves.
GOODMAN flicks on the torch he holds, and directs the
    beam around the study.)*

GOODMAN. Gloves . . . torch . . . gun . . . Now, take phone off hook. . . . (*He crosses to FORBES' desk, and removes the telephone receiver. Then:*) Unplug fridge . . . (*He crosses the room, and unplugs the refrigerator.*) What's next? Set up crank killer. . . . Find copy of "Death Game" and tear it up . . . (*He moves away towards the shelves, trips over the edge of the carpet, and falls headlong, dropping the torch.*) Blast! (*He gets to his feet, retrieves the torch, and tries to switch it on. It fails to work. He starts to bang it with his hand, as:*) Bloody torch is broke! I can't see a thing now! Find copy of "Death Game"?! I'll be lucky to find the shelves! (*He *stumbles across towards the shelves. He reaches them, and starts to search.*) I'd stand a better chance if they were all in Braille! (*He continues looking for the book. Eventually:*) It must be nearly nine fifteen . . . (*He applies the torch to his watch.*) I can't see my watch either! It was ten past when I left the car . . . it must be nine fifteen by now . . . Phone back on hook. . . . Where's the phone?! Where's the bloody desk!? (*He moves across the room, and walks into the desk.*) Found it. Replace phone. . . . (*He replaces the telephone receiver.*) Oh, this is a lovely bit of stage business, Nije — you'd love it. So long as you didn't have to be bloody well doing it! (*He reacts now as the telephone starts to ring. He panics, rushes back to the shelves, takes down a book, tears it to pieces, and throws it onto the floor.*) Get to get back over there. . . . (*GOODMAN — more clumsily than ever — blunders back across the room — hitting his shin. He just about gets to his 'killing position' when the door opens. A WOMAN enters — and is silhouetted in the doorway. She wears a fairly voluminous top coat, boots, scarf — and there is no light on her face. In the event we see her only briefly, because, as soon as she appears GOODMAN fires several shots. The WOMAN falls to lie virtually out of sight behind FORBES' desk. As she falls she grips the wall, or door jamb, and leaves behind a bloody smear from her hand.*) I did it! I did it! (*Then, in a more sombre tone:*) Oh, my God . . . I did it. . . . (*He drops the gun on the floor, turns, and runs to Exit through the french windows. The telephone rings on continuously.*)

THE CURTAIN FALLS

INTERVAL

ACT TWO

SCENE 1

*THE CURTAIN RISES ON: NIGEL FORBES' study.
    Sunday Morning.*
*The curtains at the french windows are open, and sun-
    shine streams in.*
FORBES stands by the french windows, staring out.
*The body has been removed, and along with it whatever
    blood was splashed around in the preceeding scene.
    The torn up play has gone too.*
*BERRY stands by the desk. For a few moments both men
    are utterly, grimly, immobile, then:*

FORBES. Gone forever. The old precept that an En-
glishman's home is his castle . . .

BERRY. It must have been a terrible shock for you, sir.

FORBES. Yes . . . (*He turns from the french windows,
and moves into the room.*) Utterly shocking. I knew the
man was a crank — possibly dangerous — but to return
to one's own home and to be met with . . . with *that!*

BERRY. We'll find him, Mr. Forbes. He won't get away
with it — we'll run him down.

FORBES. I hope you do. By God, I hope you do!

BERRY. (*picking up the phone*) You say this is your
business line, sir?

FORBES. Yes, it's imperative to have one clear line for
important overseas calls, that kind of thing . . .

BERRY. And, naturally it is ex-directory?

FORBES. Naturally. (*He reacts as he realises the
significance.*)

BERRY. So the amount of people who might have this
number is limited?

FORBES. I never thought of that.

(*During this exchange, we see GOODMAN appear at the french windows. He looks in — then, perceptibly 'braces himself' and arranges a smile on his face. He Enters. He still wears his anorak, and has brought in his fishing bag.*)

GOODMAN. Well . . . good morning, and a nice one too. Oh, it's you, Inspector. I saw the police car in the drive and wondered. New development in the case of the crazy crank?

BERRY. Yes, sir, I'm very much afraid there has been a new development. And a very serious one too.

GOODMAN. Oh?

FORBES. He phoned here this morning, Max — a vile and particularly obscene call!

GOODMAN. (*utterly 'thrown'*) Oh. Is that all? (*He edges across the room to deliberately peer to where the body fell. Then he turns to stare at FORBES.*) Nije . . . ?

FORBES. I didn't send for the Inspector — he arrived, quite fortuitously, with a very important clue.

GOODMAN. Clue?

FORBES. Yes, Inspector, would you mind . . . ?

BERRY. Not at all, sir — it's in the car — I'll fetch it. (*He exits through the french windows. GOODMAN instantly rounds on FORBES.*)

GOODMAN. Nije . . . !?

FORBES. Shhhh! (*He hurries to the french windows to look out, and check that BERRY has gone. He turns, as:*)

GOODMAN. Am I mad — or are you? Or is he? You're standing around talking about crank phone calls. . . .

FORBES. It actually happened. He phoned here . . .

GOODMAN. But what about the *murder?!* Where's the body?! *Where's Ann!?*

(ANN enters, and crosses to pour herself a drink. GOOD-MAN is utterly stunned, and stares at her.)

ANN. What's the matter with you? You look as though you've seen a ghost *(she gulps drink, then:)* Fernet Branca—for medicinal purposes. I feel *dead* from last night . . . *(noticing GOODMAN'S attitude)* You don't look too good either—but then you *never* look too good. *(ANN Exits. GOODMAN stares after her.)*

FORBES. *Now* do you understand? God, I had to think fast. The body's in the chest.

GOODMAN. *(turning to stare at the chest)* The body is in the . . . ? How *can* Ann be in the chest? She's there . . . I just saw her. . . .

FORBES. *(crossing to the chest, and lifting the lid)* You bloody idiot. . . .! *(He pulls JILL'S head and shoulders up into view)* You killed the wrong woman! You killed Jill! *(He reacts as he hears BERRY returning. He lowers JILL back into the chest, and closes the lid. Then he sits on the chest. GOODMAN will remain utterly dazed for some time to come. BERRY enters, holding a* large *stiff piece of card.)*

BERRY. Here we are, sir . . . *(He proffers the large card for GOODMAN to see—but GOODMAN is not seeing anything too clearly for this moment.)* It's a blow-up of the original letter. Well, sir, you see here? It's brought to light some indentations . . . where some-one has. . . .

FORBES. . . . . obviously written something else and used this piece of paper to lean on. We've used that device a dozen times ourselves.

GOODMAN. Writing?

BERRY. Block capitals. The Lab. boys assure me it says: "Rehearsal, Drill Hall, Sandown, Wednesday the fourth. . . ."

(*GOODMAN stares at him.*)

FORBES. Sandown is on the Isle of Wight, Max . . .
And Wednesday the fourth. . . .
BERRY. Was ten days before the production of "Death
Game" there.
GOODMAN. (*hesitating, then:*) I think I must sit
down. . . . (*He almost sits on the chest — then he recoils
from it — and moves to his chair at his desk. He puts his
head in his hands.*) Poor Jill. Poor, poor, Jill.
BERRY. Oh, something wrong with your secretary?
FORBES. Oh, just a migraine, nothing serious — we've
made her lie down in the dark . . .
GOODMAN. (*staring at the chest*) Yes, you could say
that . . . !
FORBES. Max. . . . !
GOODMAN. I'm all right . . . Just . . . I . . . I've
been up all night, you know.
BERRY. Oh, yes, fishing trip, wasn't it?
GOODMAN. Yes, (*still stunned*) Nije, how could I
have . . . ?
FORBES. (*hastily interjecting before GOODMAN says
too much*) Would you like a drink, Max?
GOODMAN. Yes, yes I would . . .
FORBES. How about you, Inspector . . .
BERRY. It's a bit early for me, sir. . . . (*He glances at
his watch, and raises an eyebrow. FORBES moves to
pour GOODMAN a drink, as:*)
FORBES. The Inspector has come up with a most inter-
esting theory . . . (*GOODMAN is staring at the chest.*)
Max?
GOODMAN. It's the chest there. . . . (*FORBES brings
GOODMAN his drink, and hands it over, as, warningly:*)
FORBES. *Max!*

GOODMAN. Oh, er . . . I was thinking about "Rope".

BERRY. "Rope"? By Patrick Hamilton. Yes, splendid play, sir. . . . And you're right . . . (*He taps the chest with his foot.*) Lovely place to hide a body . . .

(*FORBES moves across to the chest, and sits on it, after:*)

FORBES. *This* chest? Oh, no—one would have to *cram* a body into here . . .

GOODMAN. Nije . . . !

FORBES. You must listen to Inspector Berry's theory, Max. It may spring-board a plot development in the future. (*GOODMAN looks at BERRY.*)

BERRY. I think your crank is someone you know. Someone who worked in that company on the Isle of Wight. First we have these indentations . . . then the thorough knowledge of the play "Death Game" . . . then the fact that he called on *this* line . . . the business line . . . which is ex-directory. (*GOODMAN reacts—stares at FORBES.*)

FORBES. Yes, that was a bad mistake . . .

BERRY. And finally, the voice that spoke to you this morning, Mr. Forbes, sounded familiar.

GOODMAN. Familiar?

FORBES. It did, Max. . . . It was disguised, of course, but nevertheless it had a familiar ring.

BERRY. Which is why I have been waiting here for you, Mr. Goodman . . .

GOODMAN. What?

FORBES. The cast lists, Max. I know you type one up for every production, but I'm damned if I can recall where we file them . . .

GOODMAN. Under 'P'.

FORBES. 'P'?

GOODMAN. With the Press Cuttings. . . . (*He moves to take a file from the shelf or cabinet, and puts it on FORBES' desk ready to open it. GOODMAN suddenly notices a torn up play on the desk-top.*) Hello! Who the hell did that? (*He picks up the torn play, and studies it.*)

FORBES. What?

GOODMAN. It's our copy of "The Odd Couple" — and someone's torn it up. . . .

BERRY. Malicious damage!? Here, you don't think our crank has actually gained entrance to this house, do you. . . .?

GOODMAN. No, no, I remember now — I did it!

BERRY. Eh?

GOODMAN. I . . . I must have done. (*He bundles the torn up copy of the play into one of the drawers of FORBES' desk.*) A momentary abberation, Inspector . . . When you've . . . you've. . . .

FORBES. . . . . had your tenth rejection in a row . . .

GOODMAN. Exactly. . . .

FORBES. . . . you go ape.

BERRY. Ape?

GOODMAN. Ape?

FORBES. Ape!

GOODMAN. Right! Ape! Ape-ape-ape. And who do you turn against when you're that frustrated? The man whose *laundry* list would probably run on Broadway for ten years. Neil Simon.

BERRY. Mr. Goodman. . . .

GOODMAN. (*quickly taking a sheet of paper from the file in front of him*) Here's the credits you wanted . . .

BERRY. Oh — thank you. . . . (*He takes it.*) I'll get my men checking out these names right away . . .

Right, gentlemen . . . Good Day to you. . . . (*He exits through the french windows. GOODMAN watches him go every step of the way, then almost collapses across the desk.*)

GOODMAN. How could I have done such a thing? Jill —such a lovely girl . . . (*FORBES has made sure BERRY has gone, and now crosses to join GOODMAN.*)

FORBES. Don't you think I'm just as upset as you?

GOODMAN. *Upset*? I killed an innocent woman!

FORBES. Yes, and how on earth could you have made such a mistake? Surely you could see it wasn't Ann?

GOODMAN. That was the trouble—I could hardly see a damn thing.

FORBES. But she stood there—silhouetted . . .

GOODMAN. Exactly—*silhouetted*! The silhouette of a woman. . . . Mind you, it crossed my mind why was she wearing a coat and scarf? But I thought she'd decided to pop down to the Pub. . . . (*Then, a change of manner:*) Oh, God, Nije—what are we going to do?

FORBES. Turn our long and sometimes fruitful association to advantage . . . (*GOODMAN, who has collapsed across the desk again, slowly lifts his head to stare at FORBES.*) It will mean a rewrite. But a very small rewrite. I wish I'd thought of this earlier, Max—but I panicked. You can imagine my panic. When I came in here this morning and found all that blood, I foolishly wiped it all up—even cleaned the gun and put it away. And then compounded the felony by hiding the body . . .

GOODMAN. I would have done the same.

FORBES. No! You would have thought it through, as I am now. What do we have, Max—at this moment—what do we have?

GOODMAN. A couple of hours to flee the country?

FORBES. We have a crank on the loose—and one corpse. You didn't kill the wrong woman, Max.

GOODMAN. I didn't?

FORBES. No—our crank did . . . (*GOODMAN stares at FORBES and starts to follow his line of thought.*) Do you remember that time when Jill's car wouldn't start—so she borrowed Ann's? Well, we have to convince the police that happened again. Last night. We can pull a lead of a spark plug to disable Jill's car . . .

GOODMAN. But why?

FORBES. To make it look as though our crank killer was lying in wait to attack Ann. And he was *Jill* driving off. . . .

GOODMAN. In *Ann's* car. . . .

FORBES. Right—so he followed her and gunned her down in some remote spot.

GOODMAN. Let me get this straight. You're saying we should take Jill out of the chest—put her in Ann's car—and then drive it off the road in some woods somewhere?

FORBES. Exactly.

GOODMAN. It won't work.

FORBES. Why won't it work?

GOODMAN. Forensics, Nije—they'll check out the car and establish she was killed elsewhere.

FORBES. Not if we set light to the car and destroy it completely.

GOODMAN. I like that.

FORBES. Yes—we could collect the insurance on the car as well . . .

GOODMAN. Great! That's beautiful . . .

FORBES. I haven't told you the master touch yet. The sequel.

GOODMAN. Sequel?

FORBES. It leaves the field wide open. Our crank killer has made a mistake . . .

GOODMAN. But he's still at large.

FORBES. Exactly.

GOODMAN. So he could — he might — come back. To have another go at Ann . . .

FORBES. It's a week or two's time, when this has blown over. Weaknesses?

GOODMAN. None — except moving the body to the car.

FORBES. You can do that tonight. (*GOODMAN reacts.*) I'll take Ann down to the Pub at nine — and make sure we don't return until closing time. . . .

GOODMAN. Why me again? Isn't it about time you did some of the dirty work?

FORBES. Do you think Ann will go to the Pub with you?

GOODMAN. No, I suppose not. . . .

FORBES. Then that's settled . . . It will work, Max it will work . . . (*FORBES and GOODMAN sit down on the chest.*)

GOODMAN. Why aren't we rich, Nije? We're bloody brilliant.

FORBES. But our brilliance *is* going to bring us riches, Max.

GOODMAN. Yes . . . One thing I don't understand. Jill. Why did she come back here last night?

FORBES. I'm afraid that is something we will never know.

(*ANN Enters.*)

ANN. Still plotting?

FORBES. No, we've worked it out.

ANN. Oh—will I like it?
FORBES. I doubt it.
GOODMAN. You're so hyper-critical . . .

(*ANN is looking through the drawers of FORBES' desk.*)

FORBES. What are you looking for?
ANN. Writing paper. And I've found it. I have an important letter to write. (*She moves to the door then pauses:*) That secretary of yours—Jill—she has absolutely no system. You really should get rid of her. (*She Exits. GOODMAN and FORBES look at each other. Then:*)
FORBES. Do you think it's enough—the body found in the car?
GOODMAN. What did you have in mind?
FORBES. I don't know . . . a little added something.
GOODMAN. A cryptic note? Skin under the fingernails?
FORBES. More unusual than that . . . but obliquely relevant.
GOODMAN. Well? What do we have . . . ?
FORBES. The original letter . . .
GOODMAN. In which he accused you of being responsible for his wife hanging herself, and threatened to take his revenge.
FORBES. That's it, Max!
GOODMAN. It is?
FORBES. Hanging . . . *rope* . . . .
GOODMAN. We've already been through that . . .
FORBES. No, no—not the play—*A* rope. A symbol . . . How about a little hangman's noose?
GOODMAN. Found at the scene of the crime . . . ?
FORBES. Yes, a hangman's noose—hanging from a

nearby tree . . . There should be some string in my desk . . . (*He moves to his desk, and starts going through the drawers.*) There has to be . . .

GOODMAN. I've got some in my bag . . . (*He crosses to his fishing bag, and produces some string. FORBES pulls a length free, then tries to cut it with a paper knife, but to no avail.*)

FORBES. Damn!

GOODMAN. Don't worry, Nije . . . (*He produces his fishing knife, and cuts the twine. He watches FORBES as he tries to tie a hangman's noose.*)

FORBES. That's not right—does it go over, or under?

GOODMAN. Here, let me . . . (*He puts his fishing knife down on his desk, takes the string, and begins to fashion it into a hangman's noose. FORBES crosses to his own desk—picks up some of his neatly stacked scripts—and moves to put them on GOODMAN'S desk, scattering them carelessly—(and, in doing so, he covers the fishing knife from sight.)*)

FORBES. Now in the unlikely event that someone *should* see you coming in here tonight . . . You were checking up on early typed scripts of our plays—making sure we didn't duplicate action in the new one.

GOODMAN. Right, Nije. . . . (*He turns, and dangles a perfect little hangman's noose.*) How's that?

FORBES. Perfect . . . Now—how to shift the body?

GOODMAN. That's easy—the same way we were going to shift the bearded blackmailer . . .

FORBES. Of course, the wheelbarrow . . .

GOODMAN. You just leave everything to me. I won't get anything wrong this time.

FORBES. We must make it appear to be an ordinary Sunday. You go to the Pub . . . I'll do a spot of gardening. . . . (*He moves to a drawer, and collects some gardening gloves and secateurs.*)

GOODMAN. I'd better get going then . . .
FORBES. Yes, run along. . . .

(*GOODMAN collects his fishing bag, and Exits through the french windows. Almost immediately ANN Enters. She carries a full glass and is already on the way to being tipsy.*)

ANN. Now what are you up to?
FORBES. What does it look like? Gardening gloves. Secateurs. Sunday morning.
ANN. Oh, you're going to cut me some roses?
FORBES. Ann, you never fail me. . . . If I lay enough clues you home incisively onto the answer! And I thought, by the way, that the drink was purely medicinal . . .
ANN. *That* was the Fernet Branca. *This* is a G and T. (*She moves to start pushing buttons on the tape recorder.*)
FORBES. Now what are you doing?
ANN. I don't trust you.
FORBES. There is nothing on the tape this time. The plot is finished — finalized.
ANN. Ah, but am I still in it? (*FORBES regards her.*) The last time I played this tape I was the star of the show — worth two hundred thousand pounds. (*She laughs, drinks, and then — drunkenly:*) That's a bloody joke, isn't it? And I've always been saying, Nigel. . . . Your plays could do with a few more jokes . . . (*She turns to regard FORBES.*) Well, am I? Am I still in it? You've never used my name before, never created a character around *me*. Know why that thrills me, Nigel? Because to create a character around me, you have to look at me, examine me, know me. . . . And you haven't done that in a long, long time. (*She takes a few stumbling steps towards him, then, stops, regards him.*)

Nigel, you know I hate drinking alone. Drinking alone is so . . . lonely . . .

FORBES. (*Regards her, then nods, and moves to pour himself a drink.*) Very well.

ANN. Why don't we make a fresh start?

FORBES. Exactly what I have in mind.

ANN. (*smiles*) I'll drink to that. Fresh start. (*They drink, then:*) You didn't answer my question. The play. Am I still in it?

FORBES. Oh, yes, you're still in it, my darling. Right up to your neck!

THE CURTAIN FALLS.

Scene 2

THE CURTAIN RISES ON: NIGEL FORBES' study. Sunday Night.

The room is in darkness, and empty.

We HEAR a sound beyond the french windows, then the latch opens, and the curtain is pulled aside by GOODMAN.

GOODMAN briefly takes in the room, and crosses to his desk to switch on the lamp.

GOODMAN turns to Exit again through the french windows, but returns almost immediately negotiating a wheelbarrow into the room, and over to stand by the chest.

GOODMAN crosses back to close the french windows, and draw the curtains. He returns to the chest and regards it distastefully.

GOODMAN. God—I hope her eyes aren't open—

staring at me . . . (*The thought of this causes him to move to the drinks tray, and pour himself a glass of something. He gulps it down, then, steeling himself.*) Now come on, get a hold of yourself. It's got to be done. It's just a body — it can't hurt you. *He purposefully opens the lid of the chest — and two hands dart out and grab him round the throat! GOODMAN yells, pulls himself free, and — staggering back — has a nervous breakdown before our eyes! The hands are followed out of the chest by INSPECTOR BERRY. Without taking his eyes off GOODMAN he moves to the door — switches on the light — and calls off:*)

BERRY. Mr. Forbes!

(*Almost immediately the door opens, and FORBES Enters.*)

BERRY. You were right — he did come back.

FORBES. Oh, Max — poor Max . . .

BERRY. That's very generous, sir — after what he's done to you.

GOODMAN. (*recovering at last*) Done?

FORBES. I'm sorry, Max, I had no alternative — I had to tell him the whole story. (*As FORBES and GOODMAN talk, INSPECTOR BERRY removes the wheelbarrow, taking it out through the french windows.*)

BERRY. (*off-stage*) Constable Kingham! Take care of this.

GOODMAN. The *whole* story?

FORBES. From A to Z

GOODMAN. But why, Nije — why?

FORBES. For your sake.

GOODMAN. But it was all working so well.

(*BERRY returns, and hears the last line:*)

BERRY. No, sir — you see there was one weakness in your plan . . . a vital element you overlooked . . .

GOODMAN. No — it isn't possible . . . It was such a brilliant plan — foolproof . . .

FORBES. This isn't a play, Max. It's real life.

GOODMAN. It isn't fair. It can't end like this. *Not like this*!

BERRY. (*gently*) Mr. Goodman. *Max.* Your partner's right you know, this isn't a work of fiction . . . I know that in your mind it must be all mixed up . . . but, well . . . why don't you tell me exactly what happened?

GOODMAN. I thought *he'd* told you — from A to Z.

BERRY. Nevertheless, I'd like to hear *your* side of things . . .

(*GOODMAN hesitates — looks at FORBES — who nods, encouragingly:*)

FORBES. Go on, Max . . .

GOODMAN. Well . . . Nije, *are you sure*?!

FORBES. It can't do any harm now . . .

GOODMAN. O.K. . . . We were going to murder Ann . . . Nije?

FORBES. It's all right, Max. It's all in the open now.

GOODMAN. We were going to kill her. *I* was. Shoot her with Nigel's gun. His alibi was fixed, he spent the whole of last night at his London club. Jill had gone home — she was *supposed* to go home — and Ann was alone in the house. I got here just before nine fifteen — that's when we — *I* — had planned it. . . . (*He lapses into silence.*)

BERRY. Then what?

GOODMAN. I took the phone off the hook — unplugged the fridge — tore up our copy of "Death

Game"—except that it wasn't "Death Game" it was "The Odd Couple"—very apt!

BERRY. Then?

GOODMAN. As we planned Nije called on the business line. Ann had to come in to answer it . . . there were no lights, because of the dud bulbs . . . and she came in. But she didn't. It was Jill . . . and I shot her. I shot the wrong woman. . . . Later Nije put her body in the chest and pretended that nothing had happened, and . . . and the rest you know.

BERRY. (*Paces away in thought. Then:*) And what was the motive for this murder?

GOODMAN. Motive?

BERRY. Why did you want to kill Mrs. Forbes?

GOODMAN. The insurance . . .

BERRY. Insurance?

GOODMAN. The insurance on Ann's life—two hundred thousand pounds. We were going to split it equally, two ways, a hundred thousand each. And we were going to write happily ever after . . . Oh, damn!

BERRY. And tonight? What did you have planned?

GOODMAN. Take Jill's body out of the chest—wheel it away—dump it in Ann's car . . . and let *you* think it was the work of the crank letter writer.

BERRY. I see . . .

GOODMAN. I'm sorry, Nije. . . . I'm sorry . . .

FORBES. It's all right, Max . . . all right . . .

BERRY. It's quite a plot.

GOODMAN. But it wasn't a plot. It was *real life!*

BERRY. As *you* see it.

GOODMAN. Eh?

BERRY. (*looking at FORBES*) I think you were right . . .

FORBES. I'm afraid so.

(*GOODMAN is at a loss. BERRY bears in on him:*)

BERRY. Mr. Goodman, let me get this straight again. In that chest was the body of your secretary, Jill Prentice, whom you shot and killed last night?
GOODMAN. Yes. But you know that. It was you who moved her body, wasn't it?
BERRY. We removed the body of a woman from that chest, yes . . .
GOODMAN. Well, what else do you want—I've confessed to the crime?!

(*JILL silently Enters the room—GOODMAN is unaware of her—and remains in the background, as:*)

BERRY. I'd like an explanation for the fact that the body we removed from that chest was *not* that of Jill Prentice, but *Mrs. Ann* Forbes—and she was not shot—but stabbed to death . . . with this knife . . . (*He produces GOODMAN's knife from his pocket. It has an identifying tag attached to it.*) Your knife, I believe—it bears the initials "M.G."
GOODMAN. (*thunderstruck*) Ann? No, not Ann—you've got it all wrong. . . . The woman I killed, the woman in that chest was. . . . (*And, it is at this moment that GOODMAN sees JILL:*) Jill?! (*He is thrown for a loop again.*) She's alive!
BERRY. It's a very wonderful, spell-binding story and it's easy to see why you are a writer, Mr. Goodman.
GOODMAN. I'm not a murderer—*you're alive!*
JILL. Well, of course I am, Mr. Goodman . . .
GOODMAN. No, but you can't be. You're dead—dead and in that chest . . .
BERRY. Well, you can see for yourself that she's not

dead—and as to the other. . . . Have you ever been in that chest, Miss Prentice?

JILL. Yes

GOODMAN. You see!

JILL. Yesterday morning he and Mr. Forbes murdered me and put my body in the chest. Mind you, I was dressed as a man and wearing a beard at the time.

GOODMAN. No! Not yesterday morning—last night! You came through that door . . . you were wearing a dark coat, and . . . and some kind of head scarf. . . .

JILL. (*turning to BERRY*) I have clothes like that in my wardrobe—I'm sure most women do. But last night? I was at home watching television.

GOODMAN. Why are you lying? She's lying, Inspector.

JILL. I'm not lying, Mr. Goodman . . . and as I told you yesterday. . . .

GOODMAN. . . . You were worried about me yesterday.

JILL. Yes, I was—and I'm even more worried about you today. I tried to warn you—I've seen this breakdown coming on for weeks now. . . . I mentioned it to you several times, didn't I, Mr. Forbes?

FORBES. Yes, you did . . .

BERRY. Thank you, Miss Prentice.

JILL. (*Nods, moves to the door—then pauses, and looks sadly at GOODMAN.*) I'm so sorry . . . (*She Exits.*)

GOODMAN. This is a dream, isn't it, Nije? I'm going to wake up in a minute . . .

BERRY. I'm afraid it is very much for real, Mr. Goodman—your problem is that you're unable to distinguish fact from fantasy—which is probably how you came to make such an elementary mistake . . .

GOODMAN. Mistake?

BERRY. Elementary—and yet, I must confess it was something I completely overlooked. No, it was your eagle-eyed partner here who brought it to my attention.

GOODMAN. Nije, what's he talking about?

FORBES. Max, please do try to understand. . . . I had no choice. . . . It was my duty to phone the Inspector and tell him.

GOODMAN. Tell him what?

FORBES. That they were the same.

GOODMAN. What were the same?

BERRY. The crank letters, sir . . . and the cast list you gave me . . . and all your scripts.

GOODMAN. What about them?

FORBES. Max, soon after you left here earlier today I received a second crank letter. It had not been mailed but had been slipped under the french windows. I opened it, and sat at your desk to read it—inadvertently placing it alongside one of your typed scripts—scrutinised it closely, and then it struck me. And I immediately phoned Inspector Berry. It's probably something you haven't noticed, Max. The little 'h' . . .

GOODMAN. The little 'h'?

FORBES. On your typewriter—it is marginally out of alignment . . .

BERRY. Soon as Mr. Forbes called me I had the Lab. boys check out the crank letter I hold, against the cast list. And they matched. The little 'h'. They were both typed on the same typewriter. *Your* typewriter, Mr. Goodman. Then Mr. Forbes happened to mention he hadn't seen his wife in some hours. We became alarmed, started to check out the house, and noticed a trickle of blood here —by this chest. And then. . . . (*He gestures.*)

GOODMAN. A big twist at the end—*your* speciality— you bastard!

FORBES. Oh, Max . . .

GOODMAN. Don't bloody Max me. (*TO BERRY*) He's set me up, can't you see that . . . ?

BERRY. Mr. Goodman. . . .

GOODMAN. (*rounding on FORBES*) It was you! You sent those letters to yourself. And you used *my* typewriter . . . and there wasn't an anonymous call this morning. You crumb arse . . .

FORBES. Arse? Yes, that was one of the lesser terms of abuse he used this morning.

GOODMAN. Who used?

FORBES. The anonymous caller. (*to BERRY:*) I told you the voice had a familiar ring . . .

BERRY. (*nodding towards GOODMAN*) The same?

FORBES. Very like . . .

GOODMAN. (*Moves towards FORBES but is restrained by BERRY.*) Oh, you stinker. You . . . you absolute turd!

FORBES. *Very* like!

GOODMAN. He *has* set me up. Trapped me in my own construction . . . but I helped build it, I'll demolish it. The insurance—what about the insurance?

(*BERRY looks at FORBES.*)

FORBES. Ann was insured, yes . . .

GOODMAN. Ah *Ah*!

FORBES. A policy her mother took out . . . worth a few hundred pounds at the most.

GOODMAN. Damn you. Damn you! *The gun.* What's he done with the bloody gun, eh?

FORBES. (*Moves to open his desk drawer, and—with a sad smile—he produces the gun, and clicks the trigger.*) You will find no other gun than this. As you will immediately observe, Inspector — it is a replica incapable of firing anything other than blanks.

GOODMAN. That's how it was done! Blanks! And it *was* Jill instead of Ann. . . . Blanks . . . and she used stage blood . . . and then you briefly showed me her body in the chest, and I thought . . . (*TO BERRY*) Can't you see what's happening here? Can't you see what he's doing to me?

BERRY. I can see what you're doing to yourself, sir.

GOODMAN. Eh?

BERRY. First thing I noticed the other day — your neurotic drive. And this morning you *admitted* you suffered momentary abberations.

GOODMAN. What?

BERRY. Tearing up "The Odd Couple" . . . hating Neil Simon . . .

GOODMAN. I like Neil Simon. I worship him. "Barefoot in the Park" "The Goodbye Girl" "The Sunshine Boys". *I love the bastard*! Anyway, I only tore up "The Odd Couple" because the damn torch wouldn't work!

(*FORBES and BERRY exchange a look.*)

FORBES. You see what I mean?

BERRY. Yes, sir, I do. And it's very sad. (*FORBES and BERRY both regard GOODMAN.*)

GOODMAN. Don't look at me like that! As though I was out of my skull. As though I was a raving bloody lunatic. . . . *The noose*!

BERRY. Noose?

GOODMAN. The hangman's noose to be found beside the car — point to the crank — and muddy up the waters, eh? Ha-ha, that's something you forgot about, isn't it . . . that's something you over . . . looked . . .

(*He trails off as he suddenly touches his pocket. BERRY is quick to dart in and wrest the 'something' from GOODMAN'S pocket — it is the noose he fashioned earlier.*) Well. . . . I *was* going to plant it . . . (*to FORBES:*) But planting it didn't matter, did it? It was just a trick, wasn't it? To make absolutely sure my fingerprints were on the knife. . . . You bastard! (*GOODMAN again moves towards FORBES but BERRY intervenes. GOODMAN turns on BERRY:*) How do I know you *are* a policeman?

BERRY. Eh?

GOODMAN. How do I know? You could be his brother in disguise. How do I know that moustache is real? (*He struggles to get his hands on BERRY's moustache and pull it off, as:*) I've seen 'Sleuth' you know. Three times!

BERRY. (*Finally quells GOODMAN, and thrusts him down into a chair. BERRY stands menacingly over GOODMAN.*) Fact and fiction is all mixed up in your mind — that's how we knew you'd come back and collect the body . . .

GOODMAN. What do you mean?

BERRY. It was Mr. Forbes who pointed it out — the play you're working on. . . . Where the bearded blackmailer is murdered — put in this chest — and later the body is taken away and buried under the summer house. You see?

GOODMAN. See what?

BERRY. Fact and fiction — you can't distinguish one from the other anymore. You murdered poor Mrs. Forbes thinking she was the blackmailer. I expect that right now, in your addled mind, you think that this is a play.

GOODMAN. It is! And he wrote it! With a lot of help from me as usual!

BERRY. You're not a well man, sir.

GOODMAN. You might feel a bit under the weather too—if you were facing a life sentence!

FORBES. I don't think it will come to that, Max.

GOODMAN. You mean this is all a joke. He *is* your brother?

BERRY. That isn't what we mean at all, sir. You, er . . . probably won't even come to trial . . .

GOODMAN. Eh?

BERRY. The courts are very sympathetic towards . . . mental illness, sir . . .

FORBES. Max, it's for your own good, believe me. You've been on the verge of a breakdown for months. . . . I've tried. . . .

GOODMAN. . . . To push me over? So that's how the curtain falls, eh? I'm nuts! Well—I will be . . . if I don't figure out *why* you did this! If there's no insurance . . . then why?

BERRY. Mr. Goodman. . . .

GOODMAN. (*suddenly quite calm*) Inspector, could I have a word or two alone with you? (*BERRY and FORBES react.*) The criminal is *always* allowed a few minutes alone with the copper.

BERRY. I don't see that it can do any harm, do you, sir?

FORBES. It may help to quieten him down. I'll get Jill to make us all some coffee . . .

GOODMAN. (*as FORBES moves to the door*) But don't open the champagne for a while. You haven't got away with it yet!

(*FORBES Exits. GOODMAN settles back on the settee.*) That's nice. To hold the stage on my own for a change. Oh, begging your pardon, Inspector. . . .

BERRY. Mr. Goodman . . .

GOODMAN. I meant what I said. Nigel has to have a motive for setting me up . . .

BERRY. Mr. Goodman. . . .

GOODMAN. All right, so I'm mad — the ramblings of a lunatic. . . . But you are supposed to humour me, aren't you? He's overlooked something, I know him — he always does, and when I find it. . . . Would you like a drink, Inspector? (*BERRY reacts.*) Lager? That's your tipple, isn't it? A nice cold lager? (*BERRY stares at him.*) I'm hardly likely to get you drunk with one lager.

BERRY. Very well . . .

GOODMAN. *Moves to open the fridge door. He takes out a can of lager, and pours some into a glass, as:*) The room had to be in darkness when I did the shooting. He put dud bulbs in the lights, and then replaced them . . . (*He gives BERRY the glass and can of lager.*) I also unplugged the fridge. I wonder if he remembered that? (*BERRY has taken a sip of the lager. Now:*) Is that lager to your liking, Inspector? Ice cold, the condensation beading on the glass?

BERRY. Room temperature . . .

GOODMAN. He did forget! (*He crosses, and picks up the unplugged lead behind the fridge.*) That's one point to me, isn't it?

BERRY. One warm lager . . . ?

GOODMAN. A crack in his armour . . .

BERRY. It doesn't mean anything on its own

GOODMAN. It means I *might* know what I'm talking about . . .

BERRY. (*Regards him — his attitude just slightly altered.*) "Crazy Kill" I'll bet the shirt button was your idea . . .

GOODMAN. Not only the button but the whole damned shirt. . . .

BERRY. Found stuffed behind the hi-fi. Bit obvious. . . .

GOODMAN. That was Nigel's idea. You see what I mean, Inspector, I must still be in there with a chance when I'm dealing with a brain that can stuff a shirt behind a hi-fi! (*Reference to the hi-fi draws GOODMAN's attention to the tape recorder. He stares at it, then, turning on BERRY:*) Give me five minutes alone with him.

BERRY. Oh, I couldn't do that.

GOODMAN. Why not?

BERRY. Suppose you kill him?

GOODMAN. And eliminate the only character who knows the truth?

BERRY. No, sir, I'm sorry. . . . (*He moves to the Exit.*)

GOODMAN. Inspector, have you ever done "Gaslight"?

BERRY. (*Stops by the door, turns slowly, and is suddenly very interested.*) "Gaslight"?

GOODMAN. The Patrick Hamilton play. . . .

BERRY. Oh, yes, sir — I know the work. It's in my list of all-time favourites . . .

GOODMAN. Remember the final scene? Where Mrs. Manningham begs to be left alone with her husband — the *villain*. . . .

BERRY. And Sergeant Rough agrees reluctantly. . . . But he handcuffs Manningham to the chair first. . . .

GOODMAN. So how does that grab you? (*BERRY considers, and seems to have an inward battle, then he nods, and produces a pair of handcuffs from his hip pocket. GOODMAN moves to sit in the large chair behind FORBES' desk.*) Here I think. . . . (*He surveys the view from FORBES' chair and swings it around. Then:*) I never realised before—his chair looks down on mine. (*He picks up FORBES' spectacles which are, as always, lying on the desk. He puts them on, and mimics FORBES for a moment.*) Trust me, Max—trust me. . . . (*Then He screws up his eyes, takes the glasses off, and winces.*) Christ! His eyesight must be getting worse. (*He puts the glasses back on the desk, and regards BERRY.*) Come on then, good old Sergeant Rough . . .

BERRY. If you *were* to try and kill him . . .

GOODMAN. What with? We've established the gun only fires blanks. And this . . . ? (*He picks up the paper knife.*) He couldn't cut string with it a few hours ago . . .

BERRY. Nevertheless . . . (*He takes the knife and slips it into his pocket. He goes to put the handcuffs on GOODMAN, then has second thoughts.*) This is *awfully* theatrical, sir . . .

GOODMAN. If I am right . . . wouldn't you like to know *why* he did it? If not as a policeman, then as a student of the drama?

(*A moment, then BERRY handcuffs GOODMAN's left hand to the chair.*)

BERRY. I'll give you five minutes—no more . . . (*He moves to open the door and call out:*) Mr. Forbes!

(*During this move GOODMAN swings round in the chair, and switches the tape recorder on. A moment—then FORBES appears.*)

FORBES. Yes, Inspector?

BERRY. Now he wants to talk to you alone. If you're willing . . .

(*FORBES Enters.*)

FORBES. Very well . . .

BERRY. Five minutes, that's all you've got. I'll call the station from the car. . . . (*He crosses the room, and Exits through the french windows. FORBES moves towards the french windows, and makes sure BERRY is out of earshot. Then he turns to GOODMAN. GOODMAN regards him, then contrives, despite the handcuffs, to applaud.*)

GOODMAN. I don't know which deserves the most applause — the plot or the performance.

FORBES. The performance. . . . ? (*He gestures his hand this way and that way as though to say "So-so".*) But the *plot*. . . . I knew I'd surprise you one day . . . (*During the ensuing scene FORBES will keep a constant eye on the french windows, to make sure BERRY is in the garden and not eavesdropping. As FORBES does this GOODMAN will glance at the tape recorder to make sure it is running.*)

GOODMAN. Then you admit you set me up?

FORBES. Yes . . . between friends . . .

GOODMAN. But why, Nije, why? I would have done the murder — I went through with it — why did *you* kill Ann? I'll go mad if you don't tell me . . .

FORBES. I'll tell you something . . . it proves what I have always suspected. I don't really need you, Max, to put together the perfect plot.

GOODMAN. But why did you do what you did? You've admitted there's no insurance. What was your motive?

FORBES. Motive? Which one would you like? One—the fact that I hated Ann, and this was a quick and final way to get rid of her. Two—I intend marrying Jill. . . .

GOODMAN. Jill?!

FORBES. Yes, as you pointed out, she's an extremely attractive girl, and we have been having an extremely pleasant affair for some months now.

GOODMAN. That's a terrible cheat. You've never given any hint that there might be something going on between you.

FORBES. Initially it was to conceal it from Ann. Then we had to include you too . . .

GOODMAN. But why? I can understand you wanting to get rid of Ann, and marry Jill. I can even understand you not wanting to have to tell me there was no insurance if you'd have let me do the actual killing. But what I *don't* understand is *why*!?

FORBES. Max, over the past year or two you have become an increasing irritation to me. The wild shouting every time you *thought* you had an idea. Your dog-like affection. Your pathetic enthusiasm, and—worst of all—*"Nije"*.

GOODMAN. "Nije"?

FORBES. (*wincing heavily*) It sets my teeth on edge every time I hear it. "Nije" My name is Nigel. *Nigel*!

GOODMAN. Is that why you did it? Because of a name?

FORBES. No, no . . . that just added a spice of pleasure to doing it . . .

GOODMAN. Doing what for Chrissakes?

FORBES. You remember Posner?

GOODMAN. Posner?

FORBES. Felix Posner, that extraordinary detective we created in "Murder Has No End".

GOODMAN. Yes, of course I do . . .

FORBES. Well, a month ago, Jill took a call from Twentieth Century Fox. They want to buy the rights in that character for a television series. The contract is drawn up and only requires a signature. It's a two million dollar deal, Max—plus the usual merchandising and residuals. . . . Two million dollars payable to our partnership and to be equally shared. That is . . . (*He points to himself.*) One million for me . . . (*He starts to point at GOODMAN—then again points to himself.*) . . . and the *other* million for me.

GOODMAN. I don't get it . . .

FORBES. No, and you're not going to. That's what I just said.

GOODMAN. But you can't do that, we've got a legal agreement.

FORBES. Ah, Max . . . and that really is the *prime* motive. Excuse me . . . (*He leans past GOODMAN to open a drawer, and to produce a document. He flourishes it.*) A copy of our partnership agreement. You recall, I had it redrawn soon after taking over the running of our affairs? It's the usual stuff—shared credits, etcetera . . . but it's in the *small print* that the sting really lies—as usual, you never even bothered to read it, did you? Allow me to quote . . . (*He picks up his glasses from the desk, puts them on, and holds the document in an important manner. He then frowns as he find that he cannot see through the glasses.*) I really must collect my new glasses—I can afford them now, Max . . . (*He takes off his glasses, and puts them back on the desk.*) Briefly, our contract stipulates that should either partner be found to be suffering from a mental illness, then the other partner gets full power of attorney in all rights. Or, in plain English, if you go 'Ape' I've got you by the short and curlies.

GOODMAN. I signed that? I must be mad!

FORBES. Ah, I see you've slipped so easily into your role. Yes, Max, as from now, in the eyes of authority, you *are* mad. Weaknesses?

GOODMAN. None that I can see. (*He covertly glances towards the tape recorder as he speaks.*)

FORBES. Think it over, Max — everything fits conveniently into place. Well, that's about it . . . (*He moves to Exit, then pauses:*) Oh, there is one other thing that might amuse you. Ann was terribly relieved when I took her out to dinner last night — *and* showed some affection. She had this silly idea that we were planning to murder her. It took me some time to reassure her otherwise. To tell her that what she had heard on this tape recorder was merely you and I plotting another play. (*GOODMAN reacts.*) Yes, Max. . . . I switched it on, then foolishly forgot to erase it. Oh, but don't worry. I have taken care of it since — and learned an important lesson. Always erase, Max. Always erase . . . (*As FORBES speaks he manipulates the tape recorder to erase. He turns, smiling at the discomforted GOODMAN.*) I'll tell Inspector Berry you're ready to leave.

(*FORBES Exits. GOODMAN turns to stare at the tape recorder, and then in utter despair, puts his head in his hands. BERRY enters through the french windows, he crosses the room to pick up his raincoat from where it lies across a chair. Then moves back to the desk, to unlock the handcuffs and:*)

BERRY. Time we went. Mr. Goodman. (*And, quite casually he then picks up FORBES' spectacles from desk and as he pockets them:*)

GOODMAN. (*dull, monotone*) They're Nigel's.

BERRY. Oh, yes. (*He makes to put them back on the desk, then reacts, regards them more closely, then peers through them. Then:*)

GOODMAN. Pity they did away with hanging. I'd have preferred it. Well, it's more dramatic, isn't it? A real final curtain. Still, I suppose, if I'm coping an 'insanity plea' it makes no odds, does it?

BERRY. Your big mistake was the typewriter. The misaligned 'h'.

GOODMAN. (*gloomily nods*) The vital clue. Not exactly a show stopper — but that's Nije all over.

BERRY. Effective though. Let's see if I got it right — for the record? Mr. Forbes — Nigel — received a second crank letter — sat down at your desk to read it . . .

GOODMAN. And just *happened* to place it alongside one of my scripts — and then he noticed the misaligned . . .

BERRY. (*interjects*) No, he 'scrutinised it closely' — weren't they his exact words? He scrutinised it closely?

GOODMAN. What's it matter?

BERRY. Perhaps more than you think. (*Now BERRY searches amongst the papers on the desk until he finds the optician's card.*) You know, when I first came here the other day, I noticed this. I'm a man who notices things. A card from an optician, telling your partner his glasses are ready for collection. They usually swap this card for the glasses when you collect them — DID he get around to collecting them?

GOODMAN. (*disinterested*) No.

BERRY. You sure of that?

GOODMAN. HE didn't have the money. We're both flat broke!

BERRY. It can be easily verified.

GOODMAN. Just ask at the bank!

BERRY. (*firmly, but gently over-rides*) *That the glasses weren't collected.* I imagine they're his spare pair?

GOODMAN. Yes.

BERRY. His ONLY spare pair?

GOODMAN. Yes. For God's sake, what's this sudden fixation with. . . . ? (*He stops dead, studying BERRY'S face and:*) You're on to something!

BERRY. You said these were Forbes' glasses. They're not—they're mine. I can tell by this little nick on the frame here . . .

GOODMAN. Now wait a minute, wait a minute . . . if they are *yours.* . . .

BERRY. (*Delves into his raincoat pocket to produce Forbes' identical glasses.*) Then these must be his. I keep a spare pair at the office, so I never noticed the swap . . . if I *had* . . . (*He squints through FORBES' glasses*). . . can't see a damned thing through them! You can see where I'm leading, can't you?

GOODMAN. The misaligned 'h'?

BERRY. The most damning piece of evidence against you. That teeny little misaligned 'h' . . .

GOODMAN. That he so closely scrutinised—*this morning* . . .

BERRY. Through *my* glasses.

GOODMAN. (*A moment of jubilation for GOODMAN as he sits back and beams at BERRY—but then his manner changes as:*) No.

BERRY. What do you mean 'no'?

GOODMAN. It's a terrible clue! No self respecting dramatist would hang a man's future on *a pair of glasses*! No, I don't like it.

BERRY. It could prove your innocence.

GOODMAN. I like it! Oh, but you have to admit, it's not in the same league as Freddy Knott's key under the mat in "Dial M" . . . !

BERRY. I'm not an experienced thriller writer like you . . . I'm still learning . . . Help me.

GOODMAN. We. . . ll. . . . let's make it a bit more substantial at least.

BERRY. How about proving *when* I lost them?

GOODMAN. That's better.

BERRY. It must have been yesterday.

GOODMAN. It HAS to be yesterday to hold water. Yes, you came here . . .

BERRY. Stood by the desk there — Forbes showed me the first crank letter . . . I put on my glasses . . . then put them down here . . . Yes, I remember now! As I got ready to go, I picked up the wrong glasses . . . must have. . . .

GOODMAN. It's still pretty flimsy . . .

BERRY. It's all you've got, Mr. Goodman!

GOODMAN. I'm almost too embarrassed to use it.

BERRY. Use it!? That's the crux of the matter, how *do* we use this information, Mr. Goodman?

GOODMAN. THAT'S more like it? That's dramatic thinking. And call me Max. . . . Yes, we — YOU stumbled onto this . . . and whichever way you look at it, it IS a lousy little clue . . . but it may take *NIJE* a few years longer to work it out.

BERRY. Unless we jog his elbow?

GOODMAN. Now we're cooking, now we're thinking like a team! (*He paces away — then:*) Get Jill Prentice' back in here! (*BERRY hesitates.*) Inspector, if we are to collaborate on this, you have to go along with my wilder ideas . . . and trust me.

BERRY. (*Regards him, then moves to the open door to call:*) Miss Prentice? Could I have a word please?

(*GOODMAN settles into FORBES' chair behind the desk, as though still handcuffed. A moment later JILL enters.*)

JILL. Yes, Inspector?
GOODMAN. It's me who wants to talk to you, Jill
BERRY. (*sotto voce*) Humour him . . .
JILL. Yes, Mr. Goodman?
GOODMAN. The Inspector won't believe me when I tell him you haven't collected Nigel's glasses yet . . . (*He holds up the optician's card, and starts to show signs of distress as he speaks. JILL reacts — looks at BERRY, who shrugs profoundly.*) Well, tell him. . . . Tell him!
JILL. No, as a matter of fact, they haven't been collected yet. Why — is it important?
BERRY. (*Looks at her, implying that GOODMAN is off his rocker, as:*) Mr. Goodman seems to think so. Thank you, Miss, you can go . . .

(*JILL moves to Exit, but pauses to listen to:*)

GOODMAN. There's a weak link somewhere, and it's got something to do with Nije's glasses. . . . I know it. . . . But I don't know how . . . !

(*JILL Exits.*)

GOODMAN. There — did you see that? We've got her worried. She'll scuttle straight back and tell Nije.
BERRY. I still don't see where you're leading.
GOODMAN. Now, we leave Nije alone in here with the evidence — *having primed him first.*
BERRY. (*Regards him, then as he realizes what GOODMAN is suggesting:*) That's brilliant!

GOODMAN. (*modestly*) Good dramatic structure.

BERRY. It'll be tantamount to a confession.

GOODMAN. Yes. Oh, oh. Problem. What excuse do we have for leaving Nije alone here?

BERRY. I'm taking you out to the summer house. Well, that IS where you intended burying Mrs. Forbes, isn't it?

GOODMAN. (*admiringly*) You think fast, Inspector — stay on the plot too. Yes, that'll get us out of this set for a while — leaving the stage to . . .

(*Even as he gestures to door, so it opens and FORBES Enters. Urbane and cool as usual, but with an underlying tension. He subtly looks to where BERRY has replaced glasses (*Berry's*) on desk.*)

FORBES. Excuse me, Inspector, but will you be finished soon? I'm sure you understand, this has been a harrowing day . . .

BERRY. (*Elaborately polishes his Forbes' spectacles, twirls them before moving to slip them back into the pocket of his raincoat hanging over the chair.*) Won't be much longer, sir. We'll be off as soon as I've taken a look at the burial site.

FORBES. Eh!?

BERRY. Where he intended putting the body. (*sotto voce*) Poor demented creature. Come along, Mr. Goodman. (*And with that, he leads GOODMAN away, and both Exit through french doors. FORBES instantly runs to the windows to peer off after them, then rushes back to the desk to snatch up the glasses there. During this, JILL enters, watching as FORBES squints through glasses, reacts, and then hurries over to start delving in Berry's raincoat pocket.*)

JILL. What's wrong?
FORBES. Nothing. (*He swaps the glasses, retrieving his own from BERRY'S pocket, leaving BERRY'S in the pocket, and, calmer now, he moves back to gently place his glasses back on the desk.*)
JILL. (*during this action*) Something is wrong. It's to do with all those silly questions they asked me about your glasses . . .
FORBES. Nothing is wrong *now*. I spotted it in time.
JILL. Spotted what?
FORBES. Somehow my glasses got swapped with Berry's—been carrying them around the past twenty four hours, during which time I am supposed to have seen a misaligned 'h', the smallest of small print. (*he touches the glasses on desk*) How demeaning it would have been to be shopped by such a piddling clue! But all is well—the last loophole plugged.

(*Then, startlingly BERRY bursts in through the study door. FORBES & JILL are taken aback as he heads straight for his coat pocket as:*)

BERRY. Forgot my glasses. (*He produces them, looks through them—then turns to address the empty french windows.*) Yes, they're mine all right!

(*GOODMAN enters in a rush through french windows, almost hopping with glee.*)

GOODMAN. He did it. He did it! (*regards FORBES*) You fell for it. You swapped the bloody glasses back. I—*we*—set up a trap and you walked right into it!
BERRY. (*Moves to handcuff FORBES & JILL to each other as:*) Nigel Forbes and Jill Prentice, I am arresting

you both to further pursuance of my inquiries into the murder of Ann Forbes, and I must caution you that anything you may say . . .

GOODMAN. (*interjects*) Oh, he knows all that—we've written it a hundred times!

JILL. You fool. You incompetent old fool!

FORBES. It . . . wasn't supposed to and like this.

BERRY. (*Moves to call out of the french windows:*) Constable Kingham! (*He now urges FORBES & JILL through the french windows.*)

GOODMAN. No, it's not quite the-happy-ever-after-ending you had in mind, it is, *Nije*!?

(*FORBES winces to the name, then BERRY addresses someone just out of sight beyond the windows:*)

BERRY. Take 'em away!

(*FORBES & JILL Exit from sight. BERRY turns back to where GOODMAN is pouring them both a drink.*)

GOODMAN. Nice, crisp ending—'send 'em out with a smile'. Thanks, Inspector.

BERRY. Oh, I just happened to stumble on the vital clue. It was YOU who made it all work.

GOODMAN. With your help.

BERRY. It was a thrill, an *honour*, to collaborate with such a professional.

GOODMAN. (*regarding him*) D'you know, I think we could work together, you and me . . .

BERRY. You and *I*.

GOODMAN. With your crime knowledge—my dramatic instincts—we would make a terrific team.

BERRY. (*overjoyed*) You really think so?!

GOODMAN. Yes, but I can't keep calling you 'Inspector', what's your first name?

BERRY. Cyril.

GOODMAN. (*Puts an arm around BERRY'S shoulders and, as he starts to lead him away through french windows:*) I'd take top billing of course.

BERRY. Of course.

GOODMAN. Yes, I think we're going to get along just fine, Cy. (*He pronounces it 'sigh', and we see BERRY momentarily break step and wince to the name, and as they Exit:*)

FINAL CURTAIN.

NOTE: ALTERNATIVE LAST LINE:

GOODMAN. Yes, I think we're going to get along just fine, Cy. (*then, anxiously:*) You don't mind if I call you Cy!?

BERRY. Not at all.

GOODMAN. Good. I mean, some people can get hyper-sensitive about that kind of thing . . .

FURNITURE AND PROPERTY LIST

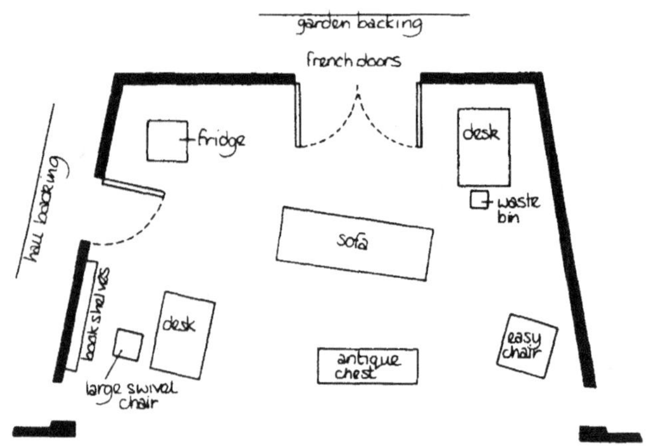

ACT I

Scene 1

On stage: Large desk. *On it:* telephone, antique desk
lamp, neatly stacked papers, antique paper
knife, electric typewriter, reading glasses,
blotting pad, card. *In the drawer:* torch,
gardening gloves, secateurs
Swing chair
Built-in shelves. *On them:* papers, books, tape
recorder, *objets d'art*
Folding-type table. *On it:* papers, jam jars
containing pencils etc., manual typewriter
Bentwood chair

94

Tin waste basket filled to overflowing
Sofa
Small fridge. *On it:* tray of bottles and glasses.
   In it: tins of lager
Antique chest
Easy chair
Framed theatrical posters
Carpet

Off stage: Tray of coffee (**Jill**)
Mail, outdoor clothes (**Ann**)
Box containing a gun and ammunition (**Forbes**)

Personal: **Forbes:** gloves
Goodman: gloves, money in pocket
Jill: false beard, snap brim hat, coat, gloves, torch

SCENE 2

Set: French window drapes drawn

Off stage: Letters (**Jill**)
Writing paper (**Jill**)

Personal: **Berry:** briefcase. *In it:* clear plastic folder

SCENE 3

Personal: **Goodman:** anorak, khaki trousers, scarf, fishing gear, gloves, torch, watch
Jill: voluminous top coat, boots, scarf

ACT II

SCENE 1

Strike: Blood from the wall

Set: French window drapes open, torn up play on Forbes' desk, file of press cuttings on the shelf

Off stage: Large stiff piece of card **(Berry)**
Glass of drink **(Ann)**

Personal: **Goodman:** fishing bag. *In it:* some string, fishing knife
Berry: watch

SCENE 2

Set: French window drapes drawn, replica gun and legal document in desk drawer, **Forbes'** glasses on his desk near his optician's card

Off stage: Wheelbarrow **(Goodman)**
Briefcase. *In it:* small bottle of green powder. Raincoat with glasses and handkerchief in pocket **(Berry)**

Personal: **Berry: Goodman**'s knife, labelled, handcuffs in pocket
Goodman: noose in pocket

LiGHTING PLOT

Property fittings required: practical overhead light and desk lamp. Fridge with working inside light

Interior. A study. The same scene throughout

ACT I

To open:	Lighting from the overhead light and desk lamp only to denote night
Cue 1	**Forbes and Goodman** *switch off lights* *Practical lights off, dim lighting only*
Cue 2	**Goodman** hurries to switch on the desk lamp *Lights up slightly*
Cue 3	**Forbes** pulls aside the french window drapes *Lights up, sunshine effect*
Cue 4	As Scene 2 opens *Dim lighting only*
Cue 5	**Jill** switches on the light *Lights up*
Cue 6	**Jill** turns out the light *Dim lighting only*
Cue 7	**Forbes** puts on the light *Lights up*
Cue 8	**Forbes** switches off the light *Dim lighting only*

Cue 9	**Forbes** draws the curtains *Light up, sunshine effect*
Cue 10	As Scene 3 opens *Dim lighting only*

ACT II

To open:	Lights up, sunshine effect
Cue 11	As Scene 2 opens *Dim lighting only*
Cue 12	**Berry** switches on the light *Lights up*

EFFECTS PLOT

ACT I

Cue 1   As the Curtain rises
           *Sounds of the countryside at night; an owl
           hooting, a rumble of thunder*

Cue 2   **Forbes:**   ". . . coming   through   the
           door. . . ."
           Car draws up outside

Cue 3   **Forbes** and **Goodman** hide
           *Door bell rings. A few moments, then it rings
           again*

Cue 4   **Forbes:** "And our audience."
           Owl and thunder noises

Cue 5   **Forbes** switches off the tape recorder
           Owl and thunder noises cease

Cue 6   As Scene 2 opens
           Telephone rings

Cue 7   **Forbes:** ". . . the phone rings. . . ."
           Telephone rings

Cue 8   **Goodman:** ". . . to get my twenty quid
           back!"
           Door bell rings

Cue 9   **Ann** pushes some buttons on the tape recorder
           Taped voices of **Forbes** *and* **Goodman**

Cue 10   **Goodman:** ". . . to be bloody well doing it!"
           Telephone rings until the Curtain falls

Cue 11   **Goodman** fires several shots
            Several gun shots

ACT II

No cues